Books by Margery Sharp

The Sun
in
Scorpio

The Sun in Scorpio

by

Margery Sharp

LITTLE, BROWN AND COMPANY

BOSTON · TORONTO

To
Geoffrey Castle

Part One

Part One

1

EVERYTHING SPARKLED.
Below the low stone wall, beyond the rocks, sun-pennies danced on the blue Mediterranean; so dazzlingly, they could be looked at only between dropped lashes. (In 1913, the pre-sunglass era, light was permitted to assault the naked eye.) Opposite, across the road called Victoria Avenue, great bolts of sunlight struck at the white stone buildings and ricocheted off the windows. A puff of dust was a puff of gold-dust, an orange spilled from a basket like a windfall from the Hesperides. Everything sparkled, from the sun-pennies on the sea to the buckles on a cab-horse's harness, from the buttons on a child's reefer-jacket to the heavy gold pendant at a girl's ear. Every-thing sparkled or shone, even the stiff black hoods of the old women; serge or alpaca, worn smooth by use, under that sun a glossy blackbird-plumage. — There were more such women abroad than usual, waiting for the Madon-na's Easter procession.

And now it came in sight: first the bouquets, rising and dipping on the tops of the long poles, each pious tribute a small rigid mound of paper roses, red and white and yellow, encircled by a gilt paper frill after the man-ner of a Victorian nosegay. (Each frill, under the Midasfinger of the sun, enriched to silver-gilt filigree.) As much did the Midas-sun for each lick of gold paint on an angel's wing, as now advanced the privileged urchin-cherubs, unnaturally clean as to face, rather strutting of gait, and scattering confetti. From under the black hoods a susurrous of grandmotherly admiration saluted them — only to die again, holily, reverentially, before the advent of the Madonna herself borne shoulder-high in blue satin and spangles under an arch of paper lilies.

All knelt.

For the three English children, Muriel, Cathy and Alan, it would have been a moment of some embarrassment, had they not known precisely what to do. — The Island, like so many other odd spots in atlases of the period, was coloured red for British: by no means so important as Malta (hence its nick-name, the Next-door Island), it nonetheless boasted a Governor, a garrison, a visit from the Bishop of Gibraltar once a year for confirmations, and in particular prided itself on being nice to the Natives. English children, even confirmed, if confronted by religious processions were strictly enjoined to preserve a respectful demeanour — never to laugh, for instance, when the Madonna's crown bobbed awry; but of course they couldn't *kneel*; so to avoid giving offence by not kneeling, the drill was to bottle into the nearest shop. In fact Muriel, at twelve, was already so expert as to have taken up a strategic position outside a toy-bazaar. (Equally instructed but less far-seeing British tots had been known to seek the unsuitable refuge of a bar.) At the precise moment before the Madonna's smiling, tolerant countenance drew level Muriel grasped six-year-old Alan by the wrist and hauled him swiftly backward into

4

Mrs. Yellow's. (Another piece of organization on Muriel's part; Alan came willingly, to look at the lead soldiers. Mrs. Yellow was so known because her shop was painted yellow.) "See the Life Guards!" exclaimed Muriel — superfluously: Alan was saving his twopence a week pocket-money with an eye to that very regiment, and with Mrs. Yellow out on the pavement took the opportunity to stroke the Drum-horse . . .

But where was Cathy, quite old enough at nine to follow under her own steam? Muriel hastened back to the door and anxiously scanned the immediate hot horizon. Kneeling adults come barely to a child's shoulders: Cathy should have been easily visible from sailor-collar up. In fact, and after some search, all Muriel could see of her was her sailor-hat. Under a sailor-hat with a ribbon round it lettered H.M.S. CROMWELL, Cathy was kneeling too.

2

The fine grit beneath her knees was all the more painful because she was still in socks. Each minute particle ground directly into bare flesh. Only a bandage round one calf, where she'd scratched a mosquito-bite till it bled, offered an approximation to a hassock; Cathy hitched it higher and let the blood flow again. Overhead the stiff black hoods closed, cocooning her in darkness: as the chant of men's voices loudened it was like sitting under the grand piano at home while Major Collier belted out "Tosti's Good-bye." Cathy notoriously wept, under the piano; she wept now, the tears dripping down her face as the blood dripped down her ankle to make a little pattern in the Island's dust.

5

Then the procession passed and she found an orange, at which insouciantly sucking Cathy rejoined Muriel and Alan in Mrs. Yellow's.

3

Major Collier was the children's mother's special Major. All the nice married Englishwomen on the Island had one — or at least a Captain, or a subaltern, or at a pinch one of the Eastern Telegraph boys: as it were a bowdlerized version of the Venetian cicisbeo; the Lion of St. Mark both corruptive of and put to shame by its successor-lion. The Venetian cicisbeo bedded his mistress in a gondola, the Anglo-Saxon, Next-door Island variety handed round scones at Sunday tea, or, like Major Collier, played the piano and sang "Tosti's Good-bye."

Cathy crouched under the instrument dissolved in tears. The threadbare warp of the drawing-room carpet bit into her knees like the grit of the street; shifting to a squat she still, through her thin Sunday knickers, suffered. But Cathy didn't mind suffering, under such glorious waves of emotion as were aroused in her by the combination of the Major's poignant shouts and the muffled thrum of felted hammers dropping directly above her head. She opened her mouth and let the tears roll in; sobs rose to meet them, almost choking her; accurately coincident with the Major's last note (uttered, by way of contrast, pianissimo), Cathy let out an uncontrollable yelp.

A big bull-terrier face stooped to her level.

"I've told you before," said Major Collier annoyedly, "do that again, and I'm going to skin you."

"Teddy, *dear!*" exclaimed Mrs. Pennon. "Frighten Cathy if you like, but please don't frighten *me!*"

6

"I crave the mem-sahib's pardon," said Major Collier.

"Or give us something more cheerful," suggested Mr. Pennon.

But all knew what to expect — the Pennons and a midshipman and a pair of E.T.C. boys — as Major Collier slammed out a series of dominant chords: a little ditty he'd composed himself.

> *Life's a pie with nothing in it,* [trolled the Major]
> > *Tooral-looral tooral-ay,*
> *Ain't we fools to want to cut it*
> > *Tooral-looral looral-ay?*

As he sang he gazed dolefully into Mrs. Pennon's eyes. Heavily chaperoned as she was, she received the look with complacency. She wasn't really a *femme fatale* any more than she was really a mem-sahib; it was in India, not on the Next-door Island, that flourished the sisters of Mrs. Hauksbee, the man-eaters, the wreckers of promising careers; India was the Empire's true hothouse, transforming home-bred mignonette to tropic orchid. Mrs. Pennon, with her fox-red hair and freckles, blossomed as it were but halfway, to a calceolaria. However, in thin lace-trimmed muslins, slotted here and there with ribbon, she presented a fragile, crushable appearance that Major Collier found definitely toothsome.

"Cynic!" chided Mrs. Pennon.

The Major, that honest bull-terrier, looked gratified. The midshipman and the E.T.C. boys, who between them had consumed some two dozen of their hostess's hot scones, had at least the manners to applaud. — It

7

wasn't the salon of Madame de Sevigné, it wasn't Mozart playing to an Archduchess, but in other drawing-rooms at the same hour mere subalterns strummed "The Teddy Bears' Picnic."

In all such drawing-rooms the chat turned mostly on the coming war with Germany. No one in either Service — Army or Navy — doubted its imminence. Westminster, the headquarters of Empire, might have a mind fixed on trouble in Ulster; the Next-door Island knew better. Supporting myths abounded: such as that a German destroyer had slipped by night in and out of Malta's Grand Harbour reconnoitring defences. Since this operation could have been far more easily performed, in daylight, by any intelligent German tourist, the destroyer was probably a myth indeed; but even myths have their significance. The Next-door Island, with its long experience of sea-fight and siege, at its point of nexus in the Mediterranean, smelled war in the air — to the extreme satisfaction of every midshipman and subaltern wolfing down their hostesses' hot scones.

4

It was all the more creditable to Mrs. Pennon to have a Major at her skirts since the Pennons' position on the Island (as she herself often laughingly remarked) was that of neither flesh nor fowl nor good red herring. They weren't Army, they weren't Navy, they were irretrievably civilian; it was a measure of Mrs. Pennon's social insecurity that she always felt nervous before giving a dinner-party in case no one came. At least they weren't Trade, however, and she made a point of explaining that her husband's chest was weak. "Doctor's orders!" murmured Mrs. Pennon, into any sympathetic (or even unsympathetic) ear. "Otherwise, of course, we'd be living on the property in Yorkshire. — Though I can't exactly see myself in *tweeds!*" added Mrs. Pennon, laughingly . . .

Actually it wasn't so much Henry Pennon's chest that was weak as his will. He wasn't precisely a remittance-man; the small income on which he and his family subsisted was his by inheritance, from a sire manufacturer of wallpapers; but it was typical of him that he'd taken the first opportunity to sell out of what was a thoroughly sound and going concern. He was a new sport, in the thriving, thrusting British middle class; a man in whom the commercial instinct (strong foundation of British prosperity) had somehow petered out — if not absolutely a renegade, certainly an odd fish. One of the advantages of having an Empire is that even the oddest fish can always find somewhere within its bounds an accommodating, low-cost-of-living pool.

5

Why Miss McCorquodale, a Scotswoman in her mid-thirties, had ever taken up residence on the Next-door Island, there to establish a private school inevitably known as Corky's, no one quite knew. She said herself it was to avoid giving pain to her aristocratic connections — the allusion not (as indeed her appearance guaranteed) to any scandal in the Divorce Courts, but to her wee pittance of a portion: the Duke in particular was such a thorough old Highland chief, he'd feel responsible for even a second cousin. — "Than which I'm no more," confessed Miss McCorquodale frankly, "and he's enough hangers-on as it is, poor soul!" The daring of this reference to a Duke as a poor soul was in general rather admired, and if no one believed in her pretensions for a

9

moment — any more than they believed in Mrs. Pennon's to a Yorkshire estate — no one, either, was unkind enough to ask when she'd last heard from His Grace. In the same way it was considered bad form to smile at the several enlarged photographs of Strathspey Castle that decorated Corky's private sitting-room. The Empire also was a clan, and whatever her antecedents Corky was accorded brevet-rank as a gentlewoman, a person to be asked to tea once a month if nobody special was expected, also to be entrusted with the education of one's children.

Corky didn't educate very far. The three R's were about her limit. Her strength lay in Manners and Self-Reliance, and not a pupil passed through her hands without learning to say, "Good morning, Miss McCorquodale," and tie its shoelaces in a bow.

Except the Baroness.

The Baroness was Italian: plump, fair-ringletted, and about ten years old. "Isn't that very young to be a Baroness?" asked Muriel rather censoriously, upon their first introduction. The Baroness giggled amiably; she was very good-natured. Her father was the Italian consul, her mother, who never appeared, a Principessa; under all these handicaps the Baroness through sheer plump good nature came smiling through. "I was born so," explained the Baroness placidly. "What a pretty necklace you have on!"

The Baroness said Good morning with the best of them, but when it came to tying her own shoelaces fell so far below the Corky standard as to be kept in at least once a week, copying out such lines as "I must learn to tie a bow." The fact that the maidservant who brought and fetched her positively strained at the leash to perform this office was to Miss McCorquodale neither here nor there. — Or rather it was *there*, as a challenge to her authority. "If I teach my pupils nothing else, I teach them self-reliance!" said Miss McCorquodale, and so the Baroness was kept in at least once a week.

All the other, English, children, headed by Muriel, thoroughly approved this discipline. Only Alan for some reason rather pitied the poor plump incarcerated Baroness, and sometimes lagged behind his sisters to look at her through the window. He wasn't alone; the Baroness's Teresa — tall as a grenadier, grim as a she-wolf of the Apennines — waited too; at the sight of Miss McCorquodale emerging for a pre-luncheon stroll Teresa literally bared her teeth. So did Corky bare her teeth, but in a pleasant smile, there being no slightest doubt as to who had the upper hand.

The small son of the Turkish Consul tied his shoe-laces with ease and abandon, but since they always came undone again earned little credit. A stray German Hochgebören (mother under some Hochgebören cloud) actually produced a new and more efficient way of tying shoe-laces — in a double knot; but of course all the other, English, children snubbed him at once. They knew as well as Corky which at that particular date in the world's history was the Ruling Race.

6

Outside Corky's the care of the young Pennons was entrusted chiefly to Carmela, a placid Island girl only some four years older than Muriel, whom the latter snubbed, and Alan loved, and who taught Cathy to eat slices of coarse dark bread smeared with oil and garlic. Of course an English nanny would have been preferable — but

11

what happened, lamented Mrs. Pennon to Mrs. Duff (R.N.), if one *did* bring one out, from Home? "My dear woman, they just marry sergeants," agreed Mrs. Duff. Mrs. Pennon glowed pleasantly at this community of opinion with her better, and went too far. "Because of course it isn't simply the *money*, with either of us?" suggested Mrs. Pennon cosily. "It certainly is with me," smiled Mrs. Duff. "With *my* two babes I'd take the risk like a shot. But being Navy, we're naturally poor as churchmice," smiled Mrs. Duff — neatly putting Mrs. Pennon back in her place.

Mrs. Duff was a particular thorn in Mrs. Pennon's flesh on the bi-annual occasion when the Pennons dined with the Governor. Like all the other women (save Mrs. Duff) Mrs. Pennon was a little over-eager for His bachelor Excellency's attention: Mrs. Duff took the line of sitting back and throwing him to the female hoi polloi. As a girl she had actually hunted with the Governor; with the Tiverton; the way she coughed out the word "hunt" was inimitable. — Cathy came nearest to it, after the single occasion when Mrs. Duff came to tea; but then Cathy could imitate a boatman selling lampouki. Her only other marked talent was for poker.

2

BECAUSE IT WAS too soon to get up Cathy lay in bed and watched spokes of light wheel across the ceiling like the ribs of an opening fan. The E.T.C. bus was passing, carrying the E.T.C. boys to their early shift: fanning out along the way beams of sun reflected from its windows. This was when the day began.

The first thing Cathy did on rising was to bandage her mosquito-bites. She was always considerably bitten about the legs, and in the bed-warmth of night she scratched; the best alleviation was handkerchieves soaked in cold water. Cathy wound them on each morning as an infantryman his puttees.

The heart of the day was the swim. On the rocks below Victoria Avenue sun struck through flesh and bone to marrow, making Cathy feel at once light-headed and heavy-limbed; by contrast, the sudden shade inside the bathing-boxes was almost cold. The bathing-boxes, painted red and white, were erected over a species of cisterns cut in the rock, and here the sun but penetrated between planks to draw long bright lines upon water almost cold too. A narrow gully led up to the open sea: and now came the spice of danger, every child knew these gullies to be dangerous because in them one might tread on a sea-urchin, even the jellyfish lining their sides — closed rubies, or gently waving mesembryanthemums — were accounted poisonous. Precautiously, in semi-darkness, Cathy felt her way up and emerged into the blue Mediterranean.

Everything sparkled. The sun-pennies on the blue water, at eye-level, merged into a single rippling sheet of cloth of gold. A wavelet breaking on a reef threw up a frill of gold lace. Cathy, supported by a pair of scarlet water-wings, turned on her back and felt the sun lap her even as the sea did.

But where the sun struck most royally of all was on the flat roof of the house. It was here Cathy took her curtailed siesta; sometimes she brought out a quilt, sometimes didn't bother but stretched equally unprotected from the heat of the stone beneath and the heat of the sun on her face. Down the sun beat and hotly, royally ravished, as Cathy opened to its embrace her small skinny frame.

2

Because it was Thursday, the day the English weeklies came in, Mr. Pennon was at the Garrison Library early. He indeed spent every morning there; essentially occupationless, he had nonetheless organized himself a routine which insulated him as much from his family as had the wallpaper-trade his laborious Victorian sire. After the morning session at the Library he lunched at the Garrison Club (of which he was an honorary member), returned home for the necessary siesta, took tea in his wife's drawing-room, and hastened back as at the call of duty to play bridge in the Club until dinner, at which only Muriel of his three children appeared. In such a routine Thursdays naturally stood out like beacons; there was always the chance that someone else might get at *Punch* first.

3

Because it was Friday Mrs. Pennon ordered fish. The Next-door Island, as has been said, always prided itself on being nice to natives, even to the extent of respecting their superstitions; also with the Fleet in butcher's meat soared sky-high, whereas a shilling bought lampouki sufficient to feed eight. — This business of housekeeping never occupied more than about fifteen minutes, but Mrs. Pennon no less than her husband confronted a full day. First she had to make up her mind which muslin to put on for a stroll along Victoria Avenue, and which of her large white muslin hats; and even when ready often found that Carmela had threaded a ribbon so carelessly, off came bodice or skirt to have the offending twist smoothed slot by slot with the head of a hairpin. Besides the stroll, the morning more often than not included a visit to Mrs. Yellow's cousin — not social, of course: Mrs. Yellow's Cousin — the name doubly anonymous, or derivative — was the Next-door Island's dressmaker, wonderfully adept at copying a Liberty model, and whose front-parlour strewn with fashion-papers was quite a rendezvous among Island ladies. (Even Mrs. Duff patronised her, in a rather blowing-in blowing-out sort of way; never lingering to gossip after a fitting, and so absolute to have that fitting on time, poor Mrs. Ramsey of the Gunners was once ejected into the parlour to wait half-tacked.) Mrs. Pennon never ordered much new

15

from Mrs. Yellow's Cousin, but paid her scot by perpetually having something altered; and since there is nothing more time-consuming than the discussion of alterations, mornings simply flew before it was time for lunch. After lunch came the necessary siesta, then dressing again (in case anyone dropped in for tea) took up more time; and what with trying to finish a novel from the Garrison Library and practising an accompaniment for Major Collier, Mrs. Pennon had really no time left.

4

Because it was Saturday, Muriel accompanied her mother to the Anglican church to do the flowers. Cathy for once trailed after them, but stopped to watch a goat. It was chewing sheet-music — certain broad tattered pages cast out by the organist — and the effect was highly curious: at one end went in the big black minims and semiquavers, from the other issued droppings so nearly identical in size, hue and shape, it was as though the animal's hyper-selective stomach digested but paper and staves. The goat wandered off; so did Cathy in its wake, leaving her mother and sister to their pious duty.

First they cut the arums that in the churchyard grew almost wild, then Muriel hastened back and forth with a can to fill the altar-vases from a tap in the vestry, then stood by with a cloth while her mother carefully placed, and displaced, and replaced the long dripping stems, to mop up the drops. Sometimes she functioned more importantly, as when Mrs. Pennon, who had once read and never forgotten that the secret of successful flower-arrangement was to employ fewer blooms than one thought looked pretty, over-compensated for her natural taste and didn't cut enough. Now, for example, though three brass vases contained but a quartet of lilies apiece, only one was left for the fourth, and by no amount of juggling could four into thirteen go with any holy symmetry . . .

"Run and cut me three more, dear," said Mrs. Pennon.

Muriel picked up the big scissors and went out again into the churchyard. At their coming it had been empty, but now there was someone there: a boy not much older than herself engaged in digging a six-by-two-foot trench. Muriel paused. To reach the nearest clump of arums she would have to pass quite close to him. — She knew perfectly well who he was; the son of a sergeant in the garrison who had so far let down the flag as to marry one of the Island girls. The sergeant had but reverted to the practice of the East India Company: Assunta Boothroyd united extreme good looks with obviously impregnable virtue; Jacko nonetheless occupied rather the position of a Poor White — as witness his freedom to pick up odd jobs of manual labour at an age when his contemporary betters were still at school. The masculine part of those betters rather envied Jacko his raffish life, but of course no properly nice child had any contact with him, and what Muriel was to do if he spoke to her she really couldn't think.

Fortunately he didn't speak to her. At least Jacko knew his place. He had inherited much of his mother's handsomeness, her black hair and black eyes; also his father's fair skin, crossed by a darker complexion, the sun had burned neither to the English pillar-box red, nor to the Islander's swarthy sallow, but to pure bronze, heading him like a faun. — With an intake of breath that heaved her muslin bosom (she was very well-developed for her age), Muriel stepped bravely by; at the moment of almost physical contact (so close to the path was Jacko digging), started as though she hadn't hitherto observed him, then with a backward flick of her heels gained the arum-clump.

It took so long to choose the three very best lilies, Muriel was forced to pause again; because the sun was so hot, had absolutely to unbutton her collar, to let a little air percolate between her unusually well-developed breasts. — How hot it was! Muriel panted. She was almost fainting, before Jacko's hands opened on the handle of his spade and he let it drop and took a first step towards her.

"Feeling the heat, miss?" asked Jacko.

"Go away, you impertinent boy!" cried Muriel; and snatching up her lilies fled back into sanctuary.

5

Because it was Sunday Cathy dusted the drawing-room. Muriel thought the task good for her, but Cathy in fact enjoyed it; she found the drawing-room so beautiful. Its main feature was a set of six white-and-gold arm-chairs, locally carved after some local, innocent ideal of elegance and luxury. They were like the chairs sat in by princesses in fairy-tale books; the arms terminated in lions' heads, the feet were eagles' claws, and the open backs wreaths of roses. Against the blue-washed walls they looked so wonderful, Cathy thought of them as Cassiopeia's Chairs floating in the sky. Equally wonderful were the four ebony panels embossed with ivory geishas; when the sun threw into sharp relief each accurately incised fold of sash and kimono, the geishas seemed almost to lean out and smile at Cathy with secret Oriental smiles. As for the Benares brass trays, under the sun they glittered like pure gold — fit for the geisha-princesses to take tea upon, if they ever stepped life-size from the walls to sit in the white-and-gold chairs. It was a scene Cathy often pictured.

6

Because Mrs. Pennon was giving a dinner-party, all the children were out in the garden helping Stella the cook make ice-cream.

The process necessarily took place out of doors owing to its elaborate messiness: involving a churn, an Army blanket, and a quantity of salt. Something went into the churn's middle compartment; was packed about with salt, lapped again in the blanket, then Stella churned. When she had to rush back into the kitchen, as happened every five or ten minutes, Muriel churned instead. Sometimes she let Cathy churn. (Alan just licked the salt.) Cathy could have churned forever, in the dark garden under the big stars. It smelled of figs and sweet-geranium, not so strongly as under the sun, but with a peculiar preciseness of each odour which Cathy in fancy herself released with each thrust at the iron handle. Rhythmically she laboured, employing all the weight of her small frame, until she rocked as she'd rocked in the sea; buoyed by the stored heat of the sun in earth still faintly warm to bare knees . . .

The fig-tree grew against a wall upon which, about a foot from the ground, certain small crosses were scratched: grubbing amongst its roots Alan once turned up the head of a china doll. The children had had predecessors, in the garden.

7

Because it was after Easter there loomed the great social event of the children's year: the Governor's Fancy-dress Ball.

3

CATHY WENT AS a Bear, in legs cut from an Army blanket, brown jersey, and headpiece fashioned from a brown plush muff mistakenly dispatched as a Christmas present to Corky and by her unloaded on Muriel as a Good Conduct prize. Alan was an Elf, chiefly identifiable by a green felt cap, and Muriel, who had been so good about giving her muff up, had a brandnew contadina costume of red sateen skirt, black velvet stays, white muslin bodice and coif.

Thus arrayed, self-consciously Contadina, Bear and Elf ascended the staircase of Government House. — It was a point of grievance amongst some of the ruling race on the Next-door Island that His Excellency absolutely refused to have his dwelling dubbed a Palace. It was nonetheless a structure of some antiquity, looming sudden and massive above the oldest street on the Island, the picturesque Strada San Giorgio, and on its seaward side fortified. Within, dim frescoes commemorated the sea-battle of Lepanto; ranked across the broad landing, suits of armour less welcomed than threatened — or might have done, had not the Governor's aide-de-camp conceived the happy thought of attaching a trio of balloons to each vizor: naturally red-white-and-blue.

The same motherly hand had got at the great saloon beyond. Irremovable, as valuable and irreplaceable Government property, between the tall windows giving upon a balcony hung taspestries commemorating not merely battles, but martyrdoms; the aide-de-camp had devoted half his morning to pinning red-white-and-blue paper fans over the more explicit disembowelments. It produced a very pretty effect, also gave the boy-guests an interest, as they surreptitiously prowled from fan to fan looking behind.

Their sisters needed no such titillation. As the saloon filled the little girls scrutinized one another with a cold ferocity of criticism that would have done credit to the quizzers in a Bath Pump-room. The standard was not so much aesthetic as conventional: contadinas and gypsies passed so to speak automatically, whereas the child in the prettiest dress of all — the thin Grecian tunic, leaving one shoulder bare, of a Wood-nymph — was universally condemned as *showing too much*. Scarcely better fared the poor Baroness, who came as a Powder-puff. This was in itself a perfectly acceptable costume, if materialized in pink or blue sateen with a band of cotton-wool round the hem: the Baroness's solecism consisted in real swansdown almost waist-high mounted on real satin. (Also ruched.) Of course she looked much more like a powder-puff than any of the other Powder-puffs; but censure was nonetheless severe.

"Really!" exclaimed Muriel. "When she can't even tie a bow!"

Upon Alan however the plump swansdowny Baroness made a rather deep impression, and he voluntarily asked her for the first dance — fortunately a polka, since this was the only dance he knew how to. He couldn't dance the second polka with her because by that time the Baroness's partners were queueing up, many of them bigger than Alan, and heavier; despite her shocking taste she did not lack for male admirers, as many a flower-girl jigging with a gypsy (there was always a shortage of boys) enviously noted. Muriel, to even greater envy, had got hold of the aide-de-camp, and stuck to him like a leech. As for Cathy, she simply raced round in circles by herself.

She didn't mind. The light and the colour and the music and the movement so went to her head, a partner pushing and pulling she would have found if anything a hobble. As dance succeeded dance her ambit widened: she raced not only round and round the ballroom but out of the door at one end and in at the door at the other. The transit across the landing was particularly enchanting — the adagio, so to speak, between scherzo and allegretto: one moment all colour, noise and motion, the next all solemn state. Faster and faster raced Cathy through the ballroom, longer and longer paused before the vizored men-at-arms; and at last absolutely halted, brown plush ears erect, to give them a fierce military salute.

"Guard this Island well!" charged Cathy solemnly — and then raced back again into the ballroom.

All this time, however, the temperature was about eighty. Cathy's costume has been described: from the waist down Army blanket, middle part jersey, from the neck up muff. On her fifth or sixth return, and just as she'd decided to join in Sir Roger de Coverley, Cathy felt definitely sickish.

Obviously she couldn't really be going to be sick, because they hadn't had tea yet. At least that last indignity would be spared her. (To be sick at the Governor's Ball was popularly believed to mark a child for life.) Perspiration nonetheless trickled down her temples. It was cold, but not refreshing. Cathy blundered her way to a window and clung to its curtain — but from pride facing the room, also achieving a fixed, desperate smile to show she was still enjoying herself. Every few moments, however, she had to stop smiling to pant; and at last was panting so regularly and fiercely, an English nanny seated nearby quite obviously (indeed aloud) suspected, even before tea, the worst.

Not so that great and good man the Governor.

"Warm, isn't it?" suggested His Excellency.

Cathy looked up a yard or so at a brown face and black moustache, and dumbly nodded.

"Well, couldn't you unhelm a bit?" suggested the Governor. "I mean, take that busby off?"

"If I did, I wouldn't look like a Bear at all," panted Cathy.

"There are times when fancy-dress becomes a burden to all of us," agreed the Governor. "I tell you what: come out on the balcony and you can take it off there and we'll both have a breather."

Since whatever the Governor told her to do must be right, Cathy staggered out beside him already fumbling with the hook at her throat. — The aide-de-camp, recognizing his chief in one of his moods, leapt to open doors already wide, and for his pains received a directive to join the dancing.

There wasn't an unengaged girl on the Island — nor, for the matter of that a married woman — who wouldn't have envied Cathy's situation as alone with His bachelor Excellency she pulled off her bear's-head and turned it inside out to air. They stood upon the seaward, the fortified side of Government House; below the marble balustrade jutted a more formidable parapet, pierced for cannon, but now overgrown by some semi-tropical liana bearing scarlet trumpet-shaped flowers. Beyond rippled the Mediterranean under a full moon: a scent of orange-blossom wafted up, in the distance a cracked bell — in a belfry, round a goat's neck? — sounded almost sweet.

"I didn't want," apologized Cathy, "to come as a Bear. I wanted to come as a Lampshade. Did you want to come as anything?"

"I've told you, I'm in fancy-dress already," said the Governor. "Only don't repeat it."

"I won't," promised Cathy.

A breeze almost cool dried her temples, lifted the released tangle of her red hair. She was feeling better already. In a couple of minutes, in fact, with a child's swift powers of recuperation, she was perfectly recovered. She still didn't want to go in. She wanted to stay outside talking to the Governor. She felt they were in sympathy.

"Aren't you glad," began Cathy conversationally, "we've an Empire the sun never sets on?"

To her surprise, the Governor appeared to meditate. For a moment she wondered whether age might have suddenly turned him deaf. He was actually in his early forties, but to Cathy old as the hills.

"Very," said the Governor at last. "We Anglo-Saxons need the sun more than most, to warm and civilize us."

"I thought it was us who civilized the others," said Cathy, surprised again.

"There are two ways of looking at everything," said the Governor. "Suppose an Indian told you it was they who taught us to wash?"

"I shouldn't believe it," said Cathy at once.

"You would be wrong," said the Governor, "and even the Indian Army admits they taught us to play polo. How's that for a civilizing influence?"

Cathy, straining to follow him, scented irony, but unlike most children was not disconcerted by it. It seemed to her that the Governor was simply telling her two things at once — exactly what she'd have to find out later, since he had fallen into meditation again. She took the opportunity to look at him more carefully; he wasn't really seven feet tall, but on the contrary rather short; his moderate height further diminished by an uncommon breadth of shoulder, against the sparkling sea he stood almost squat. Nor did he look particularly like a soldier, as Cathy knew him to have been; he looked more, she thought obscurely, and as the image imprinted itself on her memory forever, like the wise Odysseus in her *Myths of Ancient Greece*.

"We took the Sudan," said the Governor abruptly, "with Maxims against throwing-spears; yet I suppose the Sudan's better governed now than ever since the Nile ran. So it all evens out . . . But never for a moment imagine it's we who confer all the benefits. Every Benares brass tray in a Birmingham front parlour —" here His Excellency grinned a little — "is in a sense a thread to the sun. Mind you hang on to it, you young Marid!"

"I know what Benares brass is," said Cathy, "but what's a Marid?"

"A Mahommedan imp of uncommon power," said His Excellency, "who's kept me from my duties quite long enough. D'you want to put on that headpiece again?"

Cathy sighed. There is nothing children enjoy more than serious conversation with an adult. Cathy felt she

would like to go on talking to the Governor all night —
all her life — asking questions and getting Delphic answers, content not immediately to understand all he told
her, but confident of understanding before the end. But
already he looked past her, back towards the ballroom.

"Yes, please, if you can hook me," sighed Cathy.

With the greatest kindness, with his hard brown fingers, the Governor set hook to eye. As they re-entered the
ballroom the strains of Sir Roger de Coverley rose to a
climax, a last couple capered back-to-back before tea put
an end to all but sitting-down games.

"Should we join in?" suggested the Governor courteously.

It was a proposal equalled in magnificence only by Mr.
Knightly's offer to partner Harriet. Muriel would literally
have given a tooth for it. But Cathy hung back.

"Would you mind saying that again?"

"I say too much and too little," sighed the Governor.
"Did I say anything important?"

"About holding the thread to the sun."

"I say too much and too little," repeated the Governor,
"but for what it's worth, yes; always hold the thread to
the sun. — See, the dance is over."

4

THE DANCE WAS over. That same winter Mr. Pennon took his family home. He was an indolent man, but not without judgment: he judged the Island, in its expectation of war, to be very possibly right, and had no intention of being cut off from his financial base in order to watch splendid running sea-fights. ("You might have a really grandstand view, sir," encouraged the midshipman who made this suggestion. "At any rate you'd hear the firing.") Henry Pennon's essentially civilian nature enabled him to resist the temptation easily. He had indeed to encounter some slight opposition from his wife, and here found an unexpected ally in Major Collier. "Quite right, get the Mem home," barked the Major. He achieved a sort of tender bark, his eye sought Mrs. Pennon's with poignant meaningfulness; but in general Major Collier was looking almost bright. There is nothing like war for rapid promotion; Army rejoiced with Navy, and in the Navy none more than each midshipman wolfing down a last hot scone at Mrs. Pennon's Sunday tea.

To be more precise, Henry Alistair McCrimmon, subsequently drowned in the North Sea; Henry Arthur Cooke, drowned in the Channel; and William Powell, blown up with his ship off Gallipoli.

All of which names, it was the fashion of the time, pencilled upon Mrs. Pennon's Sunday tea-cloth, to be immortalized by Muriel in chain-stitch.

2

Of course all the children knew what Home was like — not from memory, but from their Christmas-present picture-books. Home was a Birket Foster landscape, a Kate Greenaway paradise of primroses, bee-hives and pet rabbits; of paddling in brooks, nutting in woods, and dancing round the Maypole. Lucky, lucky young Pennons, with such a prospect before them!

"We shan't be here next term," announced Muriel importantly, at Corky's. "We're going Home."

"Aren't you the lucky ones!" sighed Miss McCorquodale — envisioning her own heathery moors; possibly also Strathspey Castle.

Alan in a burst of sentiment presented the Baroness, as a keepsake, with one of his Life Guards that had come off its horse. She accepted it with her usual plump amiability, and with more than usual vivaciousness asked whether he would go to Court. When Alan said yes —

"How lucky you are!" envied the Baroness. "*My* family is Black — *papalissimo!*"

Cathy had no one in particular to say good-bye to except Jacko. It was he who had taught her to play poker, during long secret sessions, at siesta-time, in the cool of a bathing-hut. — It was a stern school; Jacko had been taught by his father the sergeant, and discountenanced even deuces wild. The three other young toughs, all pure-bred Islanders, never quite saw the beauty of this, but Cathy did, and Jacko as he said himself made a fine player of her; staking in fourths of a farthing, Cathy had often cleaned up as much as twopence. The parting, however, though regretful on both sides, was unsentimental.

"Just remember what I've told you," said Jacko. "Never draw to a broken straight."

Cathy promised. She would have liked also to say goodbye to the Governor, to promise that she'd always hold the thread to the sun; but the farewell was made by her mother at one of His Excellency's At Homes. "Jolly good luck!" said the Governor cheerily. "Give my regards to your young Marid!" Mrs. Pennon thought he said Mary and meant Muriel; so Cathy never received the message.

3

It was a rather rough passage home on the P. and O. boat, especially through the Bay of Biscay. All that should have been perpendicular swayed, all that should have been horizontal slanted. The fiddles set up round the dining-tables ran like little scuppers with mulligatawny. But because they were all going Home — from India, from Egypt, from Hong Kong — everyone made the best of things, and even managed to put on a farewell concert at which a Welsh soprano (governess to the daughters of a Maharajah) sang "Land of Hope and Glory." Even the third-class passengers were invited, and as Miss Llewellyn launched into the final splendid chorus one and all raised their voices, and felt their hearts lift, in genuine unison, with genuine emotion, and utter confidence.

Some three days later the Pennons were home: to settle not on any Yorkshire property but in a semi-detached villa in one of London's less expensive suburbs.

Part Two

5

EVERYTHING DRIPPED.
The skies dripped, the lamp-posts dripped, the pillar-boxes dripped and the handles of the errand-boys' bicycles. The ivy on the front of the house dripped, in the garden behind, the roof of the summer-house dripped and the derelict raspberry-canes surrounding it. Everything dripped, except when it froze.

Everything was cold. The streets were cold, it was cold on the trams and cold in the shops. A puff of breath showed on the cold air like a puff of smoke without a fire, the icy bite from the pavements penetrated leather sole and woollen stocking. It was cold in the garden, cold in the house, it was cold at rising up and lying down, it was even cold in bed. The clothes put on in the morning were cold: boots had a peculiar built-in coldness, refrigerative of the foot within. Everything was cold except chilblains, which burnt. Cathy's bandages were transferred from her shins to her knuckles.

The sun, when there was sun, didn't as on the Island bombard, it percolated. Foiled by some peculiar non-conducting atmospheric stratum — as it were a light fog-layer never entirely dissipated — light no more than heat ever struck fully home. Thus over all lay a film of immaterial dust, subtly dulling, flattening, diminishing, under which the strange looked stranger and even the familiar different. — The furniture brought from the Island, uncrated and set in place, looked different. The white-and-gold drawing-room chairs, against a subfusc wallpaper, lost all enchantment; became grotesque. The Benares brass trays, with no sun to glitter on them, looked what they were: cheap. Even the ivory geishas on the ebony panels couldn't hold their own, against a paper apparently based on rhubarb, and with no sun to animate them. Most who bring back treasures from the Levant know this disillusion. Perhaps even Lord Elgin knew it, contemplating the rescued treasures of the Parthenon set up in Burlington House.

Mrs. Pennon looked different. Her crushable muslins put aside — not only because there was no Carmela to iron and thread them, but also on account of the prevailing temperatures — she declined into serge, and with her crushable, ribbon-slotted muslins vanished the last of her attractiveness; Major Collier wouldn't have known her. Muriel and Cathy looked different, in gym-slips instead of sailor-blouses or white frocks; all Mr. Pennon's suits were too thin, and the overcoat he bought himself swamped him. Indeed their new, heavier clothing swamped them all, diminishing individuality, and as it were underlining the fact that whereas on the Island (among some few hundreds of the Ruling Race) they'd been at least petty someones, at Home (among some fifty millions) they were nobodies.

So perhaps it happened even to Lord Elgin, Ambassador to the Ottoman Porte 1802-1803, returned to take his place among his peers as a Scottish peer.

The Pennons had bad luck in returning to an uncommonly severe winter, but the impression left on Cathy at least was indelible. She once and for all dismissed the Birket Foster vision of Home as simply an adult cod, and even the coming of spring did not alter this conviction. No primroses bloomed in the hedgerows; a London suburb afforded no hedgerows. Nor did bluebells carpet the woods, for there were no woods, nor streams for paddling. The project of keeping rabbits met with disfavour, and the only time Cathy danced round a maypole was to be in a school gym, where she got her ribbon so hopelessly entangled with the next child's, she had to stand out.

6

INSTEAD OF CORKY, Muriel and Cathy now had a Head: Miss Beatrice Allen M.A. (Oxon.). It was undoubtedly a step up for them in the educational world, but the ladder was slippery, the limitations of Corky's syllabus being at a good English High-school only too swiftly revealed. Pennons M. and C. weren't even grounded, in Algebra. In Geography neither of them knew even the belts of vegetation. Muriel still made her way far the better.

Muriel enjoyed school. The reliable order of class succeeding class, the regular hierarchy from Staff through Head Girl down to Junior Prefect, soothed and engaged all the limited social sense inherited from her mother. Rapidly spotting that where prestige was to be won lay less in the fields of Maths. and Geog. than in those of hockey and English, Muriel made the hockey-team in her first term, and her essay on "Why I would like to be a School-teacher — because it is the Noblest Profession" was read aloud in class.

So did Alan enjoy school, though more raffishly. The co-educational Lower First contained several imperious beauties of an age (six to eight) at which Englishwomen most uninhibitedly seek and rejoice in male attention.

Alan was in love with two at once — an overweight blonde and a mysterious brunette: balancing a pencil between his nostrils and his upper lip, he was never quite clear which of them he was showing off to; the giggles of the blonde, the contemptuous glance of the brunette, excited him equally — as were equally excited brunette and blonde. He was not alone in such display; coeval small boys whistled through gaps in their front teeth or stood on their heads in the playground; the co-educational Lower First in fact so surged with passion, its innocent instructress, suggesting home-made Valentines as an exercise for the art-period, little guessed what flames she fed. Alan made three — one spare, so to speak, and then rather than waste it allowed himself to become additionally entangled with a newcomer who wore gold-rimmed spectacles and was the brunette's best friend.

Neither Muriel her senior nor Alan her junior were any help to Cathy, doggedly trying to hold the thread to the sun. Both seemed to have forgotten the Island entirely. "Don't you remember Mrs. Yellow?" asked Cathy once of Alan; Alan said he didn't. "Don't you remember the sun," pressed Cathy, "making sun-pennies on the sea? — Don't you remember *anything*?"

Apparently Alan didn't. The Don Juan of the Lower First, he had too much on his mind.

"Don't you remember the Governor's party?" asked Cathy of Muriel — and for once got a response.

"When you were sick into *my* muff?"

"I wasn't!" cried Cathy indignantly.

"Well, you had to go outside," reminded Muriel.

"Because the Governor asked me!" cried Cathy. "*He* didn't think I was sick! And he told me —"

But what the Governor had told her, on that balcony

overlooking the Mediterranean, she found when it came to the point impossible to repeat to such unjust, unsympathetic ears. She felt like a secret agent cut off in enemy territory, burdened with a message she couldn't transmit.

Every night before she went to sleep Cathy repeated over to herself all the words she could remember of the Next-door Island's tongue. — Neither purely Phoenician nor Arabic, and strongly laced with Italian besides English, it was in fact simply the lingua franca of the Mediterranean, which in a way made it more difficult to hold on to. Balbus built a wall in lapidary Latin; the Next-door Island tongue was more slippery, and at last all Cathy found herself able to recall was the single noun lampouki, which she repeated over and over like a charm.

— "Whatever are you muttering?" asked Muriel. At Home they shared the same room, though naturally Muriel came to bed later.

"Lampouki," mumbled Cathy.

"If you can't go to sleep, say your prayers again," advised Muriel.

Cathy turned over and buried her face in the pillow and prayed to be taken back to the sun. Sometimes, afterwards, exercising her own heathen powers as a young Marid, she managed to transfer herself back to the balcony of Government House, there to stand beside the Governor while the band played Sir Roger de Coverley . . .

2

There were of course parties at Home too. All their young friends gave them, and though Cathy didn't make any friends Muriel made dozens, and since one sister could hardly be invited without the other, Cathy came in for a fair share of Forfeits and Postman's Knock. She hated these parties even worse than she hated school.

There was never, in the first place, enough room to circulate. — Cathy wasn't aware of the word, but she knew its meaning: roughly, to run round — out through one door and in at another, freely traversing large, brightly lit apartments and landings. At the festivities to which she trailed Muriel, one was simply herded from games in the drawing-room to tea in a dining-room — both too small; moreover if the temperature in the first sometimes rose almost uncomfortably, in the dining-room it was always freezing. (Dining-rooms commonly heated by gas-fires; in Cathy's opinion never lit early enough.) The games themselves equally offended her; instead of proper dancing, which she at least liked to watch, silly charades when no one remembered the word, and, as has been said, Postman's Knock. Cathy to her relief was rarely summoned into a chilly hall — Muriel bounced in and out like a yo-yo — to receive some smudged schoolboy kiss; and if she were, instantly discouraged her suitor (or opponent, as Cathy saw it) by a kick on the shins.

What offended her most was still the competitions. It was the great era, at children's parties, for competitions; scarcely was the first charade over when down they were all sat, pencil and paper provided, to labour through poets beginning with S, flowers beginning with R, make as many words as you can out of UNDERGROUND. Cathy, at this intrusion of practically a General Knowledge Test into what should have been scenes of hospitality and gaiety, felt simply affronted. Not so had the Governor entertained his guests . . .

"Where's your little sister, dear?" asked the kind hostesses of Muriel.

"I expect upstairs," said Muriel gloomily.

"Then hadn't you better fetch her, dear, before we sit down to tea?"

So Muriel had to rush upstairs and bang on the door; and if Cathy didn't answer immediately was thrown into a dreadful quandary in case someone else was inside. But Cathy it always was.

3

After the pleasures of Christmas came the pleasures of the summer holidays: at the end of July, a visit to the seaside.

The worst part was the daily swim, and even worse than the icy plunge the waiting for a cabin, after one had bought one's ticket, under a sort of wooden cat-walk upon which the cabins opened. The temperature was always several degrees lower than outside, also as the occupants of the cabins emerged to wring out their bathing-dresses icy droplets dripped between the planks and pitted the trampled sand. One had to stand close against a white chalk cliff to avoid them, and white chalk cliffs might be Britain's bastions but they rubbed off on clothing like pipe-clay. Then eventually one climbed a rickety wooden stair (dangerous only from splinters), shrinkingly assumed a bathing-dress still damp from the day before, and at last waded into a sea so little warm or salt, all Cathy wanted was to get out again.

Muriel could now swim half a mile. Even Alan could swim a hundred yards. Cathy, deprived of her water-wings, made no attempt even to float. She went in because she had to, and got out as fast as she could, and shivered for the rest of the morning.

"You're *making* your teeth chatter," accused Muriel. "It's really hot. It's as hot as on the Island."

"Then you just don't remember," said Cathy sourly.

(She was in fact unfair. The English summer of 1914 was brilliant.)

"I'm afraid you're a very cross, ungrateful child," said Muriel sternly, "when father's brought us all here to enjoy ourselves."

"I can't help it," said Cathy.

She couldn't help it. Who that has been ravished by the sun, showered with gold like Danäe, can hope to get off scot-free?

4

"Mother."

"Yes, dear?"

"I think Cathy needs a tonic."

Mrs. Pennon grimaced. — It was a pretty grimace, the one she thought of as a *moue*; such as she'd directed upon Major Collier when he was a bad boy, and now directed less upon her daughter than upon a military-looking man who'd strolled more than once past her deck-chair. The chair adjacent was empty; the eye of the military-looking man rested on it speculatively. Mrs. Pennon, in thin muslin, under a pink-lined parasol, was feeling almost her old mem-sahib self again. Muriel however sat firmly down, and the military-looking man passed on.

"I'm sure I never heard such nonsense!" exclaimed Mrs. Pennon irritably.

"She never used to be so difficult," persisted Muriel. "I think perhaps for one thing she doesn't get enough orange-juice. On the Island she was always sucking oranges. Miss Allen says orange-juice does you more good than anything else."

"Very well, then, *buy* Cathy an orange," said Mrs. Pennon, opening her purse.

Muriel far-sightedly extracted half-a-crown, so that every morning for the rest of their stay Cathy had an orange after breakfast. She said they didn't taste the same, however, and daily discarded a half-sucked soggy mess upon the sand under the bathing-boxes, for Muriel to cover up.

Cathy hated Muriel. She saw in Muriel a renegade to the Island; a renegade to the sun.

5

The brilliant summer of 1914 was also the summer when war came, justifying at once the Next-door Island's foresight and the prudence of Mr. Pennon in bringing his family home; but also putting him to much of the financial inconvenience he'd aimed to avoid. The Pennon income, on the Island so adequate, was at Home modest to begin with; now as prices rose and his wife demanded more and more housekeeping money, Mr. Pennon seriously considered doing his bit in some paid occupation. The patriotic motive reinforced the financial: posters proclaiming that Kitchener wanted him Henry Pennon could ignore, he was over-age, nor indeed did it appear to him likely (as suggested by an almost equally famous poster) that Alan would ever enquire what Daddy'd done in the Great War: Mr. Pennon could still have served his country as a clerk in the newly-formed Ministry of Pensions, as substitute school-master, as trainee in a munitions-factory. When it came to the point, however, when he contemplated all the effort involved for the sake of a few pounds a month, he instead quietly decided to live on capital.

To prevent himself appearing occupationless, however (which at Home, at that juncture, was rather frowned upon), he embarked upon a history of British sea-power in the Mediterranean. As he had always, on the Island, been used to spend his mornings in the Garrison Library turning over papers from home, so now he spent them at the Tate Free, copying out passages from books already written on British sea-power; and Mrs. Pennon, as she'd once explained that his chest was weak, told her new neighbours that owing to his long residence in the Mediterranean her husband was quite an authority, on sea-power.

About the first thing Mr. Pennon did after deciding to live on capital was to have the drawing-room wallpaper changed. He had recognized it immediately, and with aversion, as one of the last designs he'd seen through the mill before selling out. But even against the new trellis of rambler-roses neither the geishas nor the gold-and-white chairs looked much better.

7

AS THE WAR — the Great War, the war to end wars — gathered momentum, as the casualty lists lengthened, London in the West End was reported uncommonly gay. *Thés dansants* particularly flourished, enabling debs to do their bit by foxtrotting with the brave boys from four o'clock onwards; some were still hard at it (after of course a rest period behind the lines) at the same hour next morning. This was however but hearsay to London's suburbs — proud of their brave boys but wishing they'd spend more of their leave at home. The war, in the suburbs, was a matter neither of all-night hops nor of splendid running sea-fights; it was more a general damper, like a perpetual film of immaterial dust.

At school Miss Allen's moral suasion levied a tax on all weekly pocket-money to contribute to a fund for the poor Belgians. (*Les braves Belges.*) Miss Allen felt sure the school would want to do its bit, and suggested a quarter as the appropriate amount. Cathy, who only got fourpence anyway, was as financially embarrassed as her father.

Curiously enough, from the tide of Belgian refugees there washed up at Miss Allen's school a Baroness. Unlike the Baroness of the Next-door Island she was thin and beetle-browed — also sixteen, a far more suitable age. At first she received much sympathy, even when it turned out that she'd refugeed quite comfortably in a first-class cabin; but her manners were so over-bearing, after but a couple of weeks Muriel's slamming of her down won general applause.

"Actually my little brother had a friend who was a Baroness," recalled Muriel — in much the same tone in which she'd have said that her little brother once had a rabbit. "Quite a nice child: Italian."

"Poof!" said the Belgian Baroness contemptuously. "Those Italians, anyone who has a pair of shoes is a Baroness!"

Muriel smiled.

"I see you're just like us here in England," said Muriel. "*We* think all foreign titles pretty silly too . . ."

The Baroness took the point at last. Her beetle-brows drew together; no one was surprised, or sorry, when she left at half-term for a finishing-school near Ascot. — Miss Allen in particular, who had taken her in at specially re-duced fees, never felt very warmly towards *les braves Belges* again, and transferred the weekly toll on her pupils' pocket-money to the gallant French.

3

Muriel was turning out a natural leader. Muriel was a prefect. As prefect, she impressed special squads to arrive early and dust the library, dust the studio, polish up the brass in the science lab. Miss Allen thought the world of her — as did the games-mistress: without Muriel as Captain the Junior hockey-team wouldn't have stood an earthly. "Come on, team!" yelled Muriel, with flashing eye; and the blood not infrequently trickled down Cathy's shins, pressed into service as she was, on sheer speed, as right wing.

"That child gets as whacked about the legs as a polo-pony," once observed Mr. Pennon, meditatively surveying the customary bandage bulging Cathy's long black stocking. "I think myself the forward play's getting too rough," said Muriel. "I'm going to take it up in Committee." (Of course she was on the Inter-Schools Hockey Committee as well. She was on everything.) "I mean, isn't it now particularly, while we're fighting a just war to save civilization, the time to keep Junior Hockey clean?" ("I see you have your mother's ear for a cliché," murmured Mr. Pennon.) "The trouble is that everyone knows Cathy's my sister and always bashes back."

"Instead of turning the other shin?"

"If I were able to say Cathy *didn't* bash back," pointed out Muriel austerely, "my task would be easier."

No wonder the Head thought she would make a splendid school-mistress. It was true that Muriel no more than Cathy possessed an academic brain, but then what character she had! — so much more important to the instruction of youth. Sometimes, hearing her tick off a junior, Miss Allen perceived in Muriel true vocation.

As for Cathy, she continued sour and unpopular.

She couldn't help it. Even a young Marid must feel its uncommon powers powerless against the ethos of a good English High-school; and as the sun fructifies so can it shrivel.

"Mother."

"Yes, Muriel?"

"I don't like to say it, Mother," said Muriel, saying it all the same, "but I still think Cathy needs a tonic."

Mrs. Pennon glanced impatiently up from her novel. Like her husband she had discovered the Tate Free Library, and nostalgically identifying her lost Major with Alan Quartermaine was reading straight through Rider Haggard. If Muriel thought her mother could do with a tonic too, that was something she didn't say. Like all good prefects (and politicians), she worked within the bounds of the possible.

"I think for one thing," continued Muriel, "school lunches don't agree with her. They *are* a bit starchy."

"She certainly can't come *home* to lunch," said Mrs. Pennon. "I've enough worry as it is finding something for your father to eat."

"No, but she could take sandwiches, like the vegetarians," persisted Muriel. "I'm perfectly willing to make them, Mother."

Cathy never got a tonic, but regularly every day Muriel prepared nice light sandwiches. Sometimes they were egg and tomato, sometimes egg and cucumber, sometimes sardines with cucumber or tomato. Her repertoire was necessarily limited, but she wouldn't have put in garlic even if she could have procured it; one thing Muriel did remember from the Island was how Cathy used to smell after sharing Carmela's lunch. She did her best however, day after day, week after week, with a conscientiousness and perseverance quite beyond her years.

Cathy indeed preferred sandwiches to toad-in-the-hole,

but they made her conspicuous even amongst vegetarians — a low lot in any case — because of the sardines.

5

However resolute Muriel to support Kitchener by keeping Junior Hockey clean, and though regularly if glumly Cathy shelled out a penny a week, the war passed essentially over the children's heads. Its first real impact, again rather curiously, resulted from the entirely normal, peace- or war-time, procedure of sending Alan to a proper school. At nine he could no longer accompany his sisters, co-education ceasing after the Upper First, which Alan left secretly engaged.

8

THE ESTABLISHMENT CHOSEN for him was
a local day-school self-designated, on letter-paper
and brass plate, For Sons of Gentlemen. This already,
in 1916, raised a few educated eyebrows, but Mrs. Pennon for one thought it very nice, and rejoiced that
Alan would run no danger of rubbing shoulders with sons
of tradespeople. The Head was positive on the point:
his curriculum, he explained, with a modesty that de-
ceived no one and wasn't meant to, hadn't been designed
to fit youngsters for trade. — When Mr. Pennon, present
with his wife at this preliminary interview, asked what it
did design to fit them for, the Head easily avoided a direct answer by pointing to the Roll of Honour. "Vol-
unteers all!" murmured the Head. (It was indeed the
case that the life-span of a son-of-a-gentleman second-
lieutenant, officering a volunteer army, in 1916 averaged
between five and six months.) "What a record, for so
small a school!"

"If only Alan were old enough!" sighed Mrs. Pennon.
"How proud *we* should be, to give him for his country!"
(To do her justice, this was essentially another cliché.
Even parents whose sons had enlisted with the sole mo-
tive of getting away from home spoke of giving them

for their country; the phrase put a parent so to speak in the swim.) "Wouldn't we, Henry?"

Mr. Pennon however said nothing, but continued reading the list of names in gold paint on stained oak. They weren't in alphabetical order because their bearers hadn't been slaughtered in alphabetical order; no doubt it would be rectified on the final tablets of bronze . . .

"Henry!" repeated Mrs. Pennon, more sharply.

Mr. Pennon reached the last name on the list, Arthur Drysdale (Thiepval), before turning to her.

"What did you say?"

"How proud we'd feel if Alan were old enough for us to give him for his country."

"England, our England!" interjected the Head automatically — one cliché touching off another. "The flower of the flock!"

Again Henry Pennon brooded. It was his wife who eagerly pressed Alan's claim (as though booking him in for the Roll of Honour) to the education of a son of a gentleman. He was accepted at once, though no thanks to his father; who, hitherto so blind to a recruiting-poster, the following morning set out to enlist.

No sudden bolt of patriotism had struck him. He simply felt suddenly tired of the whole shooting-match. He wanted to get out of, be done with, a world in which such slaughter took place and was accepted as proper. A man of more energy might have joined Peace Rallies, or made a nuisance of himself with placards outside the War Office; a man of greater directness might have simply committed suicide; Mr. Pennon found it easier to drift with a stream that would probably do the job for him.

His wife, when he broke his decision to her that evening, was considerably startled. There is a difference between giving a son for his country in the far future and giving a husband the very next day; Mrs. Pennon felt she had been unfairly taken at her word. Without particular affection for Henry, she was used to him; the prospect of being left alone with the house and children on her hands frightened her. When Mr. Pennon pointed out (a thought which had actually just occurred to him) that she would get a wife's allowance and possibly a widow's pension, she burst into tears. Henry Pennon was startled in turn; then not so startled; he had long suspected that such large words as "pride" and "country" were to his wife simply unreverberating arrangements of letters of the alphabet.

"At least one of us," suggested Mr. Pennon, "will be able to tell Alan what I did in the Great War."

"As if anyone took any notice of a poster!" exclaimed Mrs. Pennon angrily.

2

But apparently Alan had. As Mr. Pennon sallied forth — the cliché for once appropriate — next morning, he found a Union Jack tied to the laburnum by the front gate and Alan standing under it at the salute.

Henry Pennon paused. It seemed a moment, at least his son obviously saw it so, for some impressive valedictory. Nor was he at a loss for one.

"Always remember," said Henry Pennon, "if this war lasts until you're eighteen, I forbid you to volunteer. Wait until you're called up."

It was something of an anti-climax that he returned home neither with his shield nor upon it. Mr. Pennon was far over-age, quite apart from the fact that his chest turned out to be weak indeed; he returned home irretrievably civilian. Ridiculously (in his wife's opinion) the thing became an obsession: every recruiting-station in London grew familiar with him, also others further afield — for example in the West Country, where he'd read that recruiting lagged — and it was the periodic absence of their father that brought home to the young Pennons if not war's horrors, at least its unusualness. Muriel joined with her mother in regarding these excursions (or fugues, as a later generation of psychiatrists would have termed them) as merely frivolous; Alan still nourished a secret dream of seeing his parent ride up on a Life Guard's horse. But even in the West Country Mr. Pennon was rejected — though becoming quite a familiar figure there also.

9

"AH-HA! OUR ONE-LUNGED hero!" welcomed the M.O. robustly.

Mr. Pennon cautiously advanced into the bar-parlour of the Crown, the inn in which he was about to spend the night. The only other client besides the stout red-faced Medical Officer was a local elder silently consuming pale ale. — Mr. Pennon paused. He would have preferred to find the bar either crowded or altogether empty: in particular had no wish to renew acquaintance with one at whose hands he had so recently suffered acute physical indignity.

"Come on in and wet the King's shilling!" shouted the M.O.

"Thank you, no," said Henry Pennon. "In the first place I haven't earned it, and in the second I think you're drunk."

"If you'd my job of sending the flower of the flock to slaughter, so would you be," said the M.O., without rancour. "Sit down, and don't be a bloody fool."

Mr. Pennon sat. There seemed nothing else to do; also the small bar-parlour, cosy under low rafters, invited. Behind the counter a plump dark-haired barmaid smiled.

The M.O. was drinking whisky; Henry Pennon followed suit.

"That's better," said the M.O.

"Anyway, 'twill make you *feel* better," said the barmaid. "One thing I must say for spirits, they do the trick."

"Knock it back and have another," suggested the M.O.

"No more than two," warned the barmaid. " 'Tis rationed."

"Considering I brought you into the world with my own hands," said the M.O., "I think you might stretch a point. — Name's Milly," he added, to Mr. Pennon.

" 'Tis not, 'tis Cynthia," said the barmaid. "They just call me Milly because I'm a Bly."

"Only you don't pipe your eye, — do you, Milly?"

"But I am a fool," said Henry Pennon.

— The innocent, familiar badinage ceased abruptly; Milly and her accoucheur exchanged experienced glances. As abruptly, their relationship with each other changed also; now, they might have been surgeon and nurse.

"Come, come!" said the M.O. — much as he'd have said, say ninety-nine; a surgeon adopting the style of a family doctor, not to alarm the patient.

"Come on, tell us your life-story," invited Milly co-operatively. — "The gentleman's going to tell us his life-story," she added, to the silent Pale Ale. "And he's ever so brave, doctor's just been saying so; only one lung, and still wants to do his bit."

"No; take the easiest way out," corrected Henry Pennon.

"By a bit longabout route?" suggested the M.O. "If you mean what I think you mean."

"You've seen it before, then?" said Henry Pennon, momentarily interested.

"In forty years' practice, naturally," said the M.O. "The world is too much with us, but even Hamlet had scruples. Around here some go pot-holing."

"My Bly cousin Roger met his death in a pot-hole," recalled Milly. "Leastways so far as we know."

"Since he's been down fifteen years, it may be presumed," said the M.O., "unless he's turned into a troglodyte."

"You and your foreign diseases!" chided Milly. "Why don't you let the gentleman get on?"

"Actually," said Henry Pennon — in the cosy warmth and security of the saloon-bar: the lay confessional — "I inherited a wallpaper business."

"Lucky bugger," said the M.O.

"Which I sold out for a lump sum."

"Lucky bugger again," said the M.O.

"I'm surprised," said Milly. "You look so artistic."

"Directionless," corrected Henry Pennon. "Ambitionless. I don't know why. My father pulled himself up from setting blocks at ten bob a week. Possibly he put so much ambition into his business, there was none left for his seed."

"I've seen the same with fancy roses," said the Pale Ale unexpectedly. "One year's bloom and no growth."

"In any case, I sold out," continued Henry Pennon, "and took my wife to live abroad."

"Malta?"

"No, the Next-door Island," said Henry Pennon. "But it was a good shot. How did you guess?"

"Indian Civil have more guts," said the M.O. crudely.

"Hong-Kongers have bigger bellies. We get 'em all, re-tired about here."

"The detritus of Empire," agreed Henry Pennon. "As I see it now, life on the Island was purely artificial — if one wasn't in one of the Services."

This is where we get down to the knuckle, thought the M.O. But Mr. Pennon changed course again.

"Because for some reason, by that time I had a wife."

"It happens to the best of us," said the M.O.

"Of whom, when I married her, I knew nothing what-ever except that she played tennis and had a good skin, if slightly freckled."

"Freckles can be very attractive," said Milly. "A friend of mine with freckles married a gentleman farming his own land."

"If you mean your Bly cousin Hannah, she didn't make much of a bargain," said the Pale Ale.

"Then somehow I had three children."

"Don't come over me with your 'somehow' now!" chided Milly.

"Very well; my wife had a good skin," said Henry Pennon. "I wasn't in any sense physically defrauded. In fact, having only seen her from the neck up on a tennis-court, I was lucky."

"You were indeed," said the M.O. "Most of 'em work it off whacking balls about."

"But what I couldn't suspect," continued Henry Pen-non, "was the complete vacuity of her mind. When I sometimes used to try and imagine what it was like, in-side my wife's mind, all I could see was a sort of charity-bazaar — stalls labelled Army and Navy, the best stall of all labelled Government, and my wife wandering about

56

between with a tray of unwanted lavender-bags. Which was obviously ridiculous."

"Not at all," said the M.O. "My own wife's mind, now I come to think of it, must resemble an empty aircraft hangar."

"Usually we see quite a lot of the flying-boys," said Milly. " 'Tis quiet to-night."

"But there must be some explanation," argued Mr. Pennon.

"Let's only hope 'tisn't ops!" sighed Milly.

"I'll give it you," said the M.O. "Not so very long ago the women we'd have married — that is, supposing us our fathers — would have made their own bread. Now they get it from a bakery. That's simply the paradigm, old man. — Did I say paradigm? I must be drunk," said the M.O. "I'm always drunk when I say paradigm."

"But ever so wonderful with the old," put in Milly. "Doctor's a proper marvel at keeping the old out of Homes, so long as their legs last."

"Mine won't last much longer," said Mr. Pennon. "What were we talking about?"

"Your little ones," prompted Milly. "I hope they didn't turn out vacuous too?"

"I'd say completely," said Mr. Pennon. "Not that I know much about them. Muriel — that's the eldest — behaves like an overgrown Girl Guide. The boy isn't bright. As for Cathy —"

"Middle or youngest?" asked Milly interestedly.

"Middle," said Mr. Pennon. — "*She's* about as cheerful or intelligent as a sick pup."

Such was Henry Pennon's frank appraisal of his nearest and dearest, which only in the lay confessional of a saloon-bar, in the semi-anonymous company of an M.O., a barmaid and a Pale Ale could he ever have expressed.

"But why I did it, any of it," summed Henry Pennon, "I don't know. I can't remember. My life's gone by without my ever taking hold of it, and now I'm not even cannon-fodder."

The M.O., who saw what was coming, neatly ducked aside as Mr. Pennon with about the most violent gesture of his life chucked the dregs of a fourth whisky across the table. Milly was almost as quick with a glass-cloth: the Pale Ale withdrew unperturbed. — He'd seen a suicide in his time, at the Crown; a silly lad dangling at a rope's end from one of the very beams under which they'd just nattered, and a great shock to the then barmaid, actually Milly's aunt; but why that foolish pot-boy had hanged himself — in love, or in debt? — the Pale Ale couldn't for his life have remembered . . .

Mr. Pennon didn't hang himself. He in fact felt rather better for his confession, and if he returned to London next day nursing a hangover, nursed also a comforting memory.

Every so often he tried to enlist again, in the West Country, and regularly put up at the Crown. Milly always had a welcome for him; and the stout red-faced M.O. — gross and slightly foul-mouthed — became about the best friend he ever had.

2

In his new school Alan's character as Don Juan of the Firsts went temporarily underground. His love was now a senior prefect said, and considered by himself, to resemble Rupert Brooke; instead of balancing a pencil on his upper lip Alan displayed on the cricket-pitch with a glide to leg. "Not bad, young Pennon!" said the senior prefect, lightly buffeting him on the shoulder; Alan trembled as a bride at the bridegroom's touch, and Blanco'd the senior prefect's cricket-pads with passion. The brief infatuation did him no harm, however; he'd grown out of it almost before his love met death at Bapaume, and in due course naturally returned to the pursuit of mysterious brunettes and overweight blondes.

10

1917 WAS A bad year for ex–senior prefects; also for other-ranks prisoners-of-war in Germany. Between one Red Cross parcel and the next they subsisted chiefly on barley-soup and bread: in the transit-camp outside Karlsruhe coffee-grounds, even ersatz, were at a premium — bribed for with a wrist-watch, a ring, to chew on and fox the saliva. No one regretted this more ·than the Commandant, an elderly Prussian Major of the old school, who would greatly have preferred to be saddled with a camp of better-nourished escapers. The other-ranks British prisoners-of-war, in the camp outside Karlsruhe, lacked if not the will to escape simply the physical strength: a corporal of eighteen sat down to rest halfway up the steps to the cookhouse door. Organized sing-songs were unknown, in the camp outside Karlsruhe; only sometimes at night a wave of ironic song echoed from barrack to barrack.

> *Life's a pie with nothing in it,*
> *Tooral-looral tooral-ay.*
> *Ain't we fools to want to cut it*
> *Tooral-looral tooral-ay?*

The Commandant disliked this anthem particularly. "God Save the King," or "Rule Britannia," however subversive, he would in his heart of hearts have sympathized with: or "Land of Hope and Glory," to that splendid tune by *unser* Elgar; *tooral-loorals* struck him as . . . out of place. Chivalrously the Commandant asked himself whether he might not be listening to some sort of folk-song; unfortunately his opposite number Colonel Collier succumbed to wounds and malnutrition before the subject could be explored.

11

THE WAR PASSED over the children's heads. A Pageant of Empire (March 1918) written by the English mistress was far more important than the German offensive: Muriel, in the star rôle of Britannia, had whole speeches to recite.

> O thou, my embattled race," declaimed Muriel
>   confidently,
> *What awful destiny hast thou outfaced!*
> *See, still upon the sea thy ships do sail,*
> *Hear still the thunder of thy guns, on shore!*
> *An Empire backs thee with all might and main,*
> *Let the foe strike — and let him strike again!*

Even Cathy, but one of the Outer Hebrides, had a couplet.

"*Though small and weak I too will play my part,*" said Cathy rather disagreeably, "*slender my arm but ah how great my heart.*"

"*Not so, not so!*" cried Muriel, waving her trident.

> *Little indeed, but still to me most dear!*
> *Nurse of my pilots, men who know no fear!*

The Motherland has sailors still/ to sweep the
   mighty deep,
And keep good watch and ward o'er us/ that we
   may safely sleep
Whilst on the war-torn battlefields/ of brave
   undaunted France
At last victorious bugles cry/Advance! Advance!
   Advance!

Muriel and the English mistress were quite right. —
Suddenly the war was over, and the weekly tax on
pocket-money impressed not for the gallant French but
for the poor Germans, to build them up and make them
strong again.

However shaken, particularly by the naval fiasco of
Jutland and the casualty-lists of Passchendaele, Home
emerged still Land of Hope and Glory, mother of an
Empire on which the sun never set, a land fit for heroes
to live in — at least those who hadn't sunk their gratui-
ties into chicken-farms and were reduced to playing
bands in the street. — Such familiar itinerant entertain-
ments once known as German bands: now, after so re-
sounding a victory of British arms, the drummers and
tootlers in the streets were strictly British.

12

MURIEL MARRIED ALMOST as soon as she left school and put her hair up. It was a great disappointment to Miss Allen — also more of a surprise than it should have been, considering the way Muriel's bust strained at her gym-tunic. More understandable was the Head's ignorance of the fact that all Muriel's best friends happened to have elder brothers. Many of these found Muriel's full form and coiled hair a welcome change from the currently fashionable flat chests and Eton crops, and two in particular, Archy Maclaren in Barclays Bank, and Tommy Bamber on leave from a tea-plantation in Ceylon, embarked upon serious courtship.

Muriel wooed and coy was to Cathy even more detestable than Muriel bossy. Tangentially, Cathy disliked Mr. Maclaren at first sight, and was equally prepared to dislike his rival.

2

"This is Tommy Bamber, Mother," introduced Muriel at Sunday tea. (She'd had Archy the Sunday before. Even in the pleasurable excitement of being courted

Muriel retained her wonderful sense of fair play.) "Judith's brother."

Cathy, entering on their heels with a plate of scones,
groaned. Judith was one of her particular bêtes noires,
sugary and patronizing; but at least Mr. Bamber hadn't
towed her along. Nor was this the only favourable impression he created: as Cathy, always ham-handed,
tipped the plate and dropped a scone, with a chivalry
equal to the Governor's Mr. Bamber instantly picked it
up and not only transferred it to his own plate but ate
it. Cathy looked at him gratefully, and fancied him a
bit like the Governor altogether — much younger, of
course, and lanky, but equally brown-faced and black-
moustached . . .

"Now you must tell me all about Ceylon," Mrs.
Pennon was saying. "Is it ours?"

"Rather," said Tommy Bamber. "And the most mag-
nificent spot on earth — if you don't mind the sun."

3

Within a couple of days Cathy probably knew more
about Ceylon than Mr. Bamber. It lay off the southern
tip of the peninsula of Hindustan, situated between
5°55′ and 9°50′ N. lat. and 79°42′ and 81°53′ E. long.,
and its cession to Britain in 1802 was little more than a
formality: the Portuguese got there first, then the Dutch
turned out the Portuguese, but the British had (naturally) turned out the Dutch as early as 1796. The total
area including outlying islands was 25,332 square miles,
or more than three-quarters that of Ireland, but only in
the jungly parts unhealthy; so fertile was the rest of its
soil, five million happy natives (religion chiefly Buddhist)
cultivated not only tea but rice, rubber, coconuts and

cinnamon. Passing from the Encyclopaedia to the *Geographical Magazine,* Cathy discovered coloured photographs: long rows of brown-skinned women working among the tea, in white saris, their white teeth flashing smiles of welcome, the sun jinking (Cathy could see it jink), on their bangles. All the Englishmen in the picture wore special hats, wide-brimmed and double-crowned, explained the accompanying article, against sun-stroke.

"Have you your hat here?" asked Cathy, the first time she was able to get Mr. Bamber alone. "Your terai hat?"

"I'm afraid not," said Mr. Bamber, looking down at Muriel's kid-sister with a kindly grin, "if you want it for dressing-up. — How d'you know it's called a terai?"

"The *Geographical Magazine,*" explained Cathy. "With a double crown against sun-stroke."

Mr. Bamber grinned again, and ran a brown hand over his thick black hair.

"With a thatch like mine, I think there's a lot of nonsense talked about the sun. Personally I rather enjoy a good buffet from Old Golden Gloves."

Cathy glanced at him quickly, then away; as a woman glances at a love-letter before reading it.

"Old Golden Gloves?"

"Well, the sun," said Mr. Bamber, rather awkwardly. "It's a sort of name I've given him. You needn't repeat it."

"I won't."

"A boxing-glove, y'know. Not the six-button sort. — But I'd always see your sister wore one," reassured Mr. Bamber. "The mems put scarves round 'em and look very fetching . . ."

At that moment in walked Muriel and Archy from the tennis-club. After Tommy's equalizing Sunday-tea Muriel felt it only fair to enlist both suitors together at the job of sorting tennis-balls. The club Secretary had grown so slack, practically new match-playable balls were mixed with non-bouncers suitable only to be given to the Scouts, and Muriel and Archy carried in, and with Mr. Bamber's help carried out to the summer-house, more than a dozen boxes.

Archy Maclaren bore also a half-pound bar of milk-chocolate for Muriel's kid-sister. Sometimes he brought almond-brittle, sometimes peppermints — but never more than half-a-pound, because Muriel said that was enough. It was Muriel's splendid character quite as much as her splendid bust that attracted Mr. Maclaren. All Tommy Bamber really knew about her was that she played tennis and had a good skin.

4

Kid-sisters, at such a juncture, traditionally feel a participating interest and excitement, even if stimulated only by gifts of milk-chocolate and the prospect of being bridesmaid. To many kid-sisters it is the time of their young lives. Cathy was thrown into an agonizing dilemma.

On the one hand, she esteemed Mr. Bamber so highly, she longed to warn him what a beast Muriel really was; on the other, he suddenly, miraculously, opened a way back to the sun. — Cathy heard the promise from his own lips, only an evening or two later, as he and Muriel sat in the summer-house after tea again theoretically engaged in sorting tennis-balls.

"You wouldn't be lonely, in Ceylon," assured Mr. Bamber tenderly. *"For one thing, if you liked, you could have your kid-sister out . . ."*

Cathy, crouched in the raspberry-canes behind, stiffened like a hare in its forme. She had refrained from drawing attention to herself because she was crying; hadn't hitherto positively listened at all. But the planking of the summer-house was warped and voices easily percolated, and now, at such a vital moment to herself, she frankly strained her ears.

"Dear Tommy! How good you are!"

"I don't see how anyone could help being good to you," said Mr. Bamber, "when you're such an angel. Don't you know what an angel you are?"

Muriel giggled. Then their voices dropped, and Cathy could distinguish nothing more. She had still heard enough to keep her sleepless all night, tossed between the horns of her dilemma.

Because obviously one or other of them had to be sacrificed; herself or Tommy. Their fates it seemed interlocked, but their interests were in direct opposition: bliss, for Cathy, to be purchased only at the price of hell for Mr. Bamber. Cathy's view of her sister was probably biassed; hell was still the only word she could find adequate to describe a life-term of Muriel's company; and when she reflected that by a timely word she might as it were drag one she so esteemed back from the pit's mouth, Cathy very nearly determined on self-sacrifice.

Only in the tea-gardens long rows of brown-skinned women beckoned, the sun jinking on their bangles. The sun was so hot, you had to wear a terai hat.

Or if you didn't, having been knocked out by the sun

already, you just took another buffet from Old Golden Gloves.

On the one side was all her liking for Mr. Bamber. On the other, her own, Cathy mentally enlisted the Governor.

"Didn't you tell me yourself," argued Cathy, "Anglo-Saxons need the sun more than most? If I stay here much longer I shall probably just die . . ."

But persuade his image as she might, the Governor never more than shrugged. His brooding imaged eye seemed rather to rest on Muriel slumbering in the next bed.

"Mr. Bamber *likes* her," argued Cathy. "He thinks she's an angel."

The Governor's eyes hooded.

"Besides, after she's married to him she might improve . . ."

The image of the Governor dwindled like a shadow under the noonday sun. It was altruism that took a knock-out from Old Golden Gloves. All Cathy needed to confirm her in treachery was the assurance that it would pay off. — Next night as Mr. Bamber left after supper a kid-sister nipped out from behind the laburnum to bar his way and pin him down (as Mr. Pennon in a different sense should have been doing, but he was too idle) to his true intentions.

Cathy had waited until the front door shut; they were once again alone, under the laburnum (dripping as usual; it was a normally wet summer).

"Hello," said Mr. Bamber, naturally surprised. "Oughtn't you to be turning in?"

"Yes," said Cathy. "Only there's something I've got to ask." She hesitated, gathering courage; she was uncomfortably aware that she stood on shaky ground. To get the worst over at once — "I was in the raspberries," added Cathy, "behind the summer-house . . ."

Just as she'd expected, Mr. Bamber scowled.

"If you eavesdropped you were a dishonourable little brat — and if you do it again I'll skin you."

"Only I didn't," Cathy defended herself. "I didn't even listen, at first; I just heard. — Would you truly, if you married Muriel, have me to stay?"

There was a brief pause. Cathy employed it to prepare in her mind what was practically a short essay on "Why I Want to Live in Ceylon." She got in both history and geography, also her special aptitude for being hot and her expertise with mosquito-bites. She felt in fact ready to answer any question a tea-planter might reasonably put not only with assurance, but with eloquence.

"Are you as fond of your sister as all that?" asked Mr. Bamber tenderly.

Cathy blinked. For a moment it seemed to her a complete change of subject. It was a moment before she perceived his drift, another before she realized the depth, length and breadth of his besottedness. She thought fast, however, and sensibly reached the conclusion that there was no future (in Ceylon) in explaining that she hated Muriel more than anyone she knew.

"Well, we've never been separated in all our lives," said Cathy.

"And you can't bear to be now?" asked Mr. Bamber, more tenderly still.

Cathy wiped away a tear. It was actually a drip from the laburnum, but her situation excused the deceit. — Mr. Bamber, who had hitherto never seen Muriel's kid-sister as anything but Muriel's appendage, discovered in himself almost an affection for her. It crossed his mind that he'd quite like to have her running round the bungalow. But he no less than Cathy kept his eye on his own ball.

"If I promise, will you put in a good word for me?"

"It must be more than a promise; it must be a solemn pact," said Cathy sternly. "Will you make it a solemn pact that if you marry Muriel I'm to come and stay with you in Ceylon?"

It increased her esteem of him that Mr. Bamber was evidently not one to take a solemn pact lightly. He reflected.

"Not straightaway. When people get married they want to be by themselves for a bit. Then there's your education. How old are you?"

"Sixteen," said Cathy.

Mr. Bamber regarded her with momentary surprise. In her gym-tunic hanging lank from her shoulders — her hair pushed back behind her ears, her nose shining like a bone — she looked much younger; he'd always thought of her, so far as he thought of her at all, as being about twelve.

"Your people will want you to stay at school at least two more years," said Mr. Bamber. (He'd been going to say, six.) "But as soon as you're through, I give you my word of honour, and make a solemn pact, that we'll come home on long leave and fetch you. — Does it seem so long," added Mr. Bamber compassionately, and seeing tears now perfectly genuine beginning to trickle down Cathy's cheeks, "to be parted from her?"

"Ages," said Cathy. "Ages and ages . . ."

"But I can't make a solemn pact on false grounds," argued Mr. Bamber — winning her esteem all over again. "And I tell you what: if you like I'll send you a Tamil word-book and you can pick up a bit of the lingo in advance. It'll be a sort of —"

"Thread to the sun," said Cathy recklessly; and to Mr. Bamber's surprise from trickling tears burst into a storm of weeping.

— Yet he wasn't, after a moment, really surprised; wasn't the prospect of being separated for two years from such a sister as Muriel enough to make any kid cry?

6

So Cathy never warned Mr. Bamber, however much she liked him, what a beast Muriel really was; but instead, falsely faithful to her own side of their solemn pact, whenever she could drew Muriel's attention to his merits. "I think Mr. Bamber's very good-looking," said Cathy. "I think he's almost as good-looking as Jacko was." "Jacko?" repeated Muriel sharply. "That boy on the Island we weren't to speak to," reminded Cathy. "I don't remember him at all," said Muriel. It was nonetheless that same evening (again in the summer-house) that Tommy Bamber, holding her gingerly in his arms, felt for the first time a slight responsive pressure; as her lips slightly opened, his searching tongue for the first time tasted honey. — Nothing came of it, however; in the event Muriel opted not for the sun but for security. Actually she had never much liked the sun; by far preferred the respectable shades of Barclays Bank; and some six months later Cathy and Alan were to follow her up the aisle as she plighted her troth to Archy Maclaren.

Alan wore a hired kilt, Cathy her party frock and a wreath of heather. It smelled slightly of fish; the supply sentimentally ordered by Mr. Maclaren from Scotland having gone astray in the post, the only other heather immediately available decorated a salmon at the local fishmonger's. For a bridal bouquet this provenance put it out of court, nor did gardenias make an unacceptable substitute; but Muriel could be sentimental too, and marrying a braw Scot as she was, insisted on a touch of heather somewhere. The blooms decorating the chancel were of course arum-lilies.

Thus the solemn pact between Cathy and Tommy Bamber might as well have never been made. — Doubly so; since had Muriel indeed become Mrs. Bamber instead of Mrs. Maclaren she would certainly have abrogated it. In Muriel's view, Cathy was a little beast.

7

A little beast desolate and disconsolate; a little beast curling in upon itself like an armadillo. Ironically enough, Cathy missed Muriel just as much as she'd led Tommy Bamber to believe she would. An object of thorough hatred is at least an interest in life.

13

CURLED IN UPON herself disconsolate, Cathy during her last two years at school but scrambled into the Lower Sixth and stuck there, and was dropped from the hockey-team, and finally failed to pass her Matric. Like Muriel she left at eighteen, but unlike Muriel with no immediate prospect of matrimony. The latter had indeed left several fish a-swim in the Pennon waters, but Cathy was no angler, and even had she wished to be, as she did not, her hook was singularly unbaited. She still looked unnaturally young — not fresh and plumply young, but skinny-young; and not fashionably skinny, but skinny like a skinned rabbit. Nor did she look any better out of a gym-tunic than in one; if Muriel and Mrs. Pennon had long settled down into their heavier, Home-style clothing, whatever Cathy wore retained a curious knack of never seeming to belong to her. — Of course some items really didn't belong to her, in the sense that they had belonged to Muriel first, but she had new clothes as well; the trouble was that they weren't designed to be surmounted by a pale tense face and a crest of rough red hair. Only a very great dressmaker, a future Balenciaga, could have done anything with Cathy, and then the result would have been striking; as it was, she looked only too striking for an escort's comfort. Even Mr. Pennon was once moved to comment on his younger daughter's appearance, observing detachedly that it was a pity she couldn't wear a burka.

Cathy, with no prospect of matrimony, had in fact no prospect at all save the traditional one of daughter helping at home. — This in the 'twenties was still a recognized rôle, though with variations from an earlier image. A whole generation of cook-generals after doing their bits in a factory had downed aprons for ever; daughters helping at home no longer merely arranged flowers and wrote out menus, they did half the work of a house. In general they were a sulky lot, and Cathy was amongst the sulkiest. It was very hard on Mrs. Pennon, but she had developed such a technique of losing herself in a novel, a daughter's obvious misery disturbed her no more than a husband's equally obvious lack of any will to live. Alan also (practising his leg-glide and now in love with a blonde at Woolworth's) made out comfortably enough; but during the years immediately following Muriel's marriage the home-nest she had quitted could be most shortly, with accuracy, described as a good place to have got out of. Muriel never admitted the disloyal thought; she was nonetheless always glad to return, after the every-other-Sunday visit, to the new nest shared with Archy and now Baby Anna.

Cathy for her part saw the Maclarens leave as she saw them arrive; with indifference. There was slightly more washing-up, otherwise their visits but marked the passage of fortnights, then of months, then finally of some three years before any event occurred to quicken her indifferent spirits.

2

"Henry!" exclaimed Mrs. Pennon, looking up from her paper at the breakfast-table with unusual vivacity. "Henry! Who do you think is Home?"

"Our brave boys from Cologne," said Mr. Pennon bitterly.

"No; the Governor!" said Mrs. Pennon. "*Our* Governor, from the Island! — It says it here: '*Sir Rowland March, K.C.B.*' —"

"He's gone up a step," observed Henry Pennon. "They must have retired him early."

"*— in the course of an interview given in London at St. Anne's Mansions —*"

"What does he say, in his interview?" enquired Henry Pennon.

"I haven't read it," said Mrs. Pennon impatiently, "but don't you think I should *call?* I mean, though it's ten years, we were really such *friends*, on the Island! Don't you think I ought to call?"

For an instant there again floated through Mr. Pennon's mind the image of his wife peddling lavender-bags at a charity-bazaar.

"Why not? He must have learnt to protect himself," said Henry Pennon.

Mrs. Pennon chose to ignore the reflection, as she had taught herself to ignore the greater part of what went on around her; and in any case suddenly found unexpected support.

"When?" said Cathy.

It was so long since Mrs. Pennon had paid a really proper call, besides a new spring hat she needed to buy a new pair of white kid gloves; all her old ones, even kept in tissue-paper, had yellowed. So had her visiting cards, at least those on the top of the little pack, but a few towards the middle remained presentable: Mrs. Pennon selected the freshest-looking, and on the back (for after all it *was* ten years), pencilled a tactful little reminder. "*Your old friend from the Island!!*" wrote Mrs. Pennon — the second exclamation-mark, she felt, giving just the right air of gay confidence. Then she turned her attention to her daughter, whose company she was indeed in two minds about; for though it was perfectly correct, rather the done thing, to take a daughter calling with one, not, thought Mrs. Pennon obscurely, if that daughter looked like Cathy . . .

Cathy however didn't look nearly so bizarre as usual. Though she had dressed with care she still had the air of wearing someone else's clothes, but with colour in her cheeks her hair looked less startling; her eyes were bright, her expression was becomingly excited. "Why can't you always look like that?" complained Mrs. Pennon — at once relieved and annoyed. Cathy didn't answer. She could hardly tell the truth, it wouldn't have been understood, that at last, after how many desolate years, she again felt a twitch on the thread to the sun.

What Cathy hoped from the coming visit could hardly have been put into words at all. At twenty-one she was still childish enough to imagine the Governor suddenly taking her aside and dispatching her back to the Island on a secret mission; also sufficiently adult to recognize such a dream for the dream it was. What continued to brighten her eyes and flush her cheeks, in the bus that bore herself and her mother towards St. Anne's Mansions, was essentially the prospect of at last unbosoming herself. Simply to tell the Governor how she'd tried, how she'd remembered his words, receive praise, perhaps encouragement — but essentially to break silence at last — such was all Cathy hoped, and it so sufficed that for the first time in her life (her cheeks so red, her eyes so bright), she was whistled at by a youth at the bus-stop. — He had a look of Jacko; black-haired and dangerous. Cathy descending behind her mother recklessly smiled back, and scarcely noticed, as they approached St. Anne's Mansions, how diminished was the Governor's dwelling from the keep he'd once dubbed Mon Repos.

His flat was on the sixth floor. To reach it, in the slow old lift, took eternity.

4

At least the Governor still had a manservant. (Like the boy at the bus-stop an echo from the Island: stocky and black-avised, on whose breath Cathy smelled garlic.) He wore a white linen jacket, not absolutely spotless any more than the small Benares brass card-tray he produced was absolutely shining. Any steward on a P. and O. boat could have given him points. But at least he was a manservant, and Mrs. Pennon had never really expected a proper butler; she placed her card on the tray and as he withdrew sank happily down, in a graceful, mem-sahibish attitude, on the lobby's single chair. — Cathy recognized with pleasure arms terminating in lions' heads, feet carved like eagles' claws; evidently the Governor too had brought home treasure from the Next-door Island. Nosing round the walls she discovered several recognizable photographs: one of Strada San Giorgio, and one of Government House taken from the seaward side where a balcony jutted from the ballroom . . .

"How lost he must feel, poor man, without an aide-de-camp!" observed Mrs. Pennon, beginning to chat already. "I wonder if there's any little thing I could do for him — like shopping? He's sure to have an account at the Army and Navy; and when it comes to sheets probably doesn't know linen from twill!"

The door re-opened. Suddenly, just as she'd done at the Ball, Cathy felt slightly sick.

5

It didn't matter, however, because the Governor wasn't at home. The manservant returned positive: His Excellency was not at home. "What a pity!" murmured Mrs. Pennon — retrieving the pasteboard and carefully turning down one corner to show she'd called in person. "He'll be so sorry to have missed us!"

Descending in the lift neither mother nor daughter spoke. The disappointment was indeed almost as keen to Mrs. Pennon as to Cathy; that is, as keen a disappointment as she was capable of. There was even a certain nobility about it. Mrs. Pennon hadn't gossiped in advance of her impending visit. She had no humble-pie to eat. Her snobbery was so pure, the act of calling on an ex-Governor K.C.B. was precious and fulfilling in itself. So was its frustration all the more painful; Mrs. Pennon was hit at her deepest level of feeling. In the lift, descending, with a gesture for her as violent as her husband's chucking of a dregs of whisky across a table, she stripped off her new white kid gloves, and rolled them into a ball, and dropped them on the lift's dirty floor.

6

Outside in the street again Cathy suddenly halted and looked up. High upon a balcony — one of half-a-dozen, iron-railed about eight or nine square feet — she saw, could have sworn to it, the figure of the Governor gazing down. He looked much older, now, and grizzled; he stood hunched like a hawk, and what his gaze rested on wasn't the blue Mediterranean but the approaches to a railway-station. But he hadn't lost his brooding poise, indeed his hawk-look accentuated it, as of the wise Odysseus, and Cathy still recognized him.

"Don't you remember me?" called up Cathy desperately. "I was a Bear, I was a young Marid, I'm Cathy!"

But the rumour of traffic drowned her voice. From his six-storeys-up narrow balcony the Governor turned back into his narrow six-storeys-up quarters: a man used to governing islands and territories, now on the retired-list and glad of his pension, but who had learned to protect himself.

14

EIGHT THOUSAND MILES away in Ceylon, Tommy Bamber, thumbing along his shelves for something he hadn't read four or five times already, dislodged a Tamil word-book; after a moment's thought carried it to his desk and prepared to inscribe on its fly-leaf, *"To the kid-sister."*

Then he thought again. He was a young man of some perception, when not besotted by love, and recognized that the disregard, so to speak, of Cathy's personal individuality, might hurt her feelings. So he put instead, *"To Cathy, from her friend Thomas Bamber."* It was easy to remember the address.

Then, upon further reflection still, the thin package made up, he didn't send it. At the back of his mind, his perceptiveness working retrospectively, was an idea that Cathy'd not only wanted to be with her sister, but had also wanted badly to come out to Ceylon. This being now obviously impossible, mightn't the gift merely exacerbate her disappointment? Percipiently, regretfully (for he didn't like to think of anyone so fond of Muriel being unhappy), Mr. Bamber ripped the packet open again and put the pamphlet back on the shelf.

15

MR. PENNON LIVED just long enough to see a grand-daughter toddle. In the summer of that same year his will-power finally gave out and he succumbed to complications following influenza. He died, as he had lived, alone. Mrs. Pennon, who had nursed him devotedly in spite of not feeling very well herself, was out shopping; Muriel, standing guard, was in the kitchen making a cup of tea to give the doctor momentarily expected, and Cathy had been delegated to attend Alan's last cricket-match. None of them had anything to reproach themselves with. On the contrary, it seemed almost as though Henry Pennon deliberately chose that moment of solitude to slip his mortal coil — but the circumstance was nonetheless painful. "How *like* your father!" sobbed Mrs. Pennon uncontrollably. "Hush, mother!" murmured Muriel. "The doctor says now Cathy and Alan can see him . . ."

Reluctantly Mr. Pennon's son and younger daughter, caught and informed by Muriel as they came in, approached the bed; stood and stared uneasily, like a couple of colts at a sheep on its back.

"There's nothing to be afraid of," encouraged Muriel, "if you want to kiss him . . ."

To set an example she pressed her own lips to the cold paternal forehead. She never wore much lipstick, but even so a slight pink smear recorded her piety. Alan drew back; but Cathy, as she'd done on the hockey-field, followed her sister's lead — and then at the contact with icy skull-stretched skin burst into tears.

"He's so cold!" wailed Cathy. "He's so cold!"

"He'll be warm in Heaven," comforted Muriel, as though to a child. It indeed struck her even at that moment how dreadfully childish Cathy still was. "*Why, at her age,*" thought Muriel, "*I'd been married to Archy for years!*" She felt something gone amiss with Cathy; her sister's growth not only physical but emotional somehow stunted. "She's never forgotten the Island," thought Muriel suddenly. — This was a rare feat of imagination on Muriel's part; she did not pursue the train of thought, however; indeed felt almost ashamed of allowing her mind so to wander, at such a moment, to the living in the presence of the dead.

"You must be brave," added Muriel bracingly — her old perfect-self again — "and a comfort to Mother."

Mrs. Pennon needed comfort. When it came to bidding her husband a last farewell, she was genuinely distressed at the short list of guests. (It was much the same feeling, though of course heightened, as she'd experienced before giving a dinner-party on the Next-door Island.) However Muriel inserted a notice in two daily papers (*The Times* and *Telegraph*), with "all friends welcome at the church," and they could only hope for a decent dressing of at least the front pews.

2

Every death brings its revelations: as slightly disturbing
as a legacy to a Cat's Home instead of to the Lifeboat
Fund, or apt to fee lawyers for years disputing the
claims of a second domestic hearth. The revelation attending the death of Mr. Pennon fell somewhere between: that is, he left everything to his wife, but Milly
came to the funeral.

She had to take two days off to do it, sleeping the
night at her sister's in Paddington; but having slept with
Mr. Pennon every night he could get back to the Crown
(after they'd slept together that first night), saw it not
only as a duty but as a right. She brought with her the
best floral tribute of all, supplied by the Pale Ale who
happened to be a market-gardener producing floral tributes as a side-line: it was shaped like an anchor, and
upon Mr. Pennon's coffin quite outshone his wife's and
the Maclarens' simple wreaths and Cathy's simple sheaf.
These were actually the only other floral tributes at all;
the undertaker had promoted Milly's anchor from professional pride, and the latter was surprised herself at the
effect it made. She'd expected more of a funeral altogether; she truly hadn't wished to be conspicuous, but
with so very few people in church felt it would look
silly to sit behind a pillar . . .

"I say," murmured Archy Maclaren.

"Hush, dear!" murmured Muriel.

"Who the deuce sent that anchor?"

"Hush!" repeated Muriel, kneeling; and out of the side
of her mouth added resourcefully, "perhaps someone we
knew in the Navy."

Milly wept enjoyably throughout. (Which was one

thing, she told her sister afterwards, about a C. of E. service: it never let you down.) Her round rosy face, as she traditionally clasped the widow's hand in the porch, was blubbered but enthusiastic; she pressed Mrs. Pennon's hand so hard, their black kid gloves reciprocally squeaked.

"It said in the paper, all welcome," explained Milly, "also I shall ever remember your lost one as the most perfect gentleman 'twas ever my pleasure to know."

She cried all the way home, and would have gone on crying all night, had not her sister and brother-in-law sensibly taken her to a music-hall.

3

Neither Mrs. Pennon nor the Maclarens ever referred to this incident. — That is, the Maclarens never referred to it to Mrs. Pennon, though Archy in bed that night with Muriel suddenly remarked, out of the blue, that he thought better of his father-in-law than ever before. "I don't know what you're talking about," said Muriel. — "No, darling, not to-night! Not just after the funeral!"

As for Cathy, she was unaware of any incident at all. She had knelt all through the service: and grinding her knees into the threadbare hassock, almost hooded by her mother's black skirts — hearing Archy's voice rumbling out a hymn overhead — at her father's funeral knelt once again on the gritty pavement of Victoria Avenue.

4

It was more than possible that Mrs. Pennon never suspected her husband's infidelity; her own death some months later almost certainly wasn't due to a broken heart, but again, quite simply and certifiably, to complications following influenza. She truly hadn't been feeling very well, just as her husband had truly had a weak chest; also influenza, if not the scourge it had been in 1918, in that year thrust out a last grasp of its skeleton hand. Even quite young persons, after neglecting it, succumbed to it; so did middle-aged Mrs. Pennon. Fortunately she wasn't present to witness obsequies even in comparison with her husband's rather hugger-mugger. Without advertisement, followed by but four mourners, was the coffin of Mrs. Pennon lowered on top of her husband's. The floral tributes were now but two — one from Cathy and Alan, one from the Maclarens: the undertaker looked at them despisingly. However Muriel made an opportunity to inform him that Mrs. Pennon had lived chiefly abroad. "On the Island, the church would have been *crowded*," said Muriel. (Which was true, any social event on the Next-door Island so rare.) "Also please see, this time," added Muriel severely, "that there are only family wreaths on the coffin . . ."

She needn't have bothered. No exotic tribute of orchids or gardenias appeared, to disconcert with any hint of a double life on the part of Mr. Pennon's relict. (Major Collier, to do him justice, had he been alive and informed would have weighed in with at least gladioli; but Major Collier was dead too.) As the undertaker observed to his colleague, it was a very simple ceremony indeed; so also were the funerary baked meats — Cathy, expectant of the Maclarens back to lunch, having but bought a lettuce and opened four tins of sardines.

In a sense this economy was justified. Mrs. Pennon hadn't lived long enough to grasp the further revelation that in leaving her all her husband in fact left her nothing. His capital had just lasted out his own life-time, and he'd never thought to take out any sort of insurance policy. Idle, irresponsible to the end vanished Henry Pennon from the world's business — again, from his own point of view, choosing the moment that suited him.

Now it was that Muriel's wonderful sense of responsibility showed at its best.

"Don't worry, dear," said Muriel, as she and Cathy washed their hands together afterwards, "I've talked it all over with Archy; and you're to come and live with *us*."

5

Cathy sat down on the edge of the bath. Her hands still dripped; Muriel sympathetically passed a towel. To postpone the moment of full realization, before this prospect of her future —

"What about Alan?" asked Cathy.

He was really little more than a red herring; but Muriel nodded approvingly.

"You needn't worry about Alan either, dear. Of course Archy's been thinking about Alan ever since poor father died, and he can get him into the Bank. — Not in London, I'm afraid, but at quite a good branch in the Midlands, where Archy knows the manager, who's promised to keep an eye on him and find him nice motherly digs. Archy's been really wonderful," said Muriel fondly. "What we should all do without him I really can't think!"

Nor could Cathy think. That was the trouble. She had no alternative to offer, to this sudden exiling of a brother to motherly Midland digs. For a moment the wild notion crossed her mind that he and she might simply run away together, escape, become a pair of tramps, working their way south to the sun again. But she doubted Alan's willingness, for wasn't he too a renegade? — as Muriel's next words indeed proved.

"I expect they're talking about it now," said Muriel comfortably. "Of course Archy spoke to Alan first — and he really seems to enjoy the idea, of being *independent!* The only point —"

"But there must be *some* money," interrupted Cathy. So fast does thought fly, she simultaneously abandoned Alan to his horrible but chosen fate and saw herself with just enough cash to get back to the Island and start a school like Corky's. "There must be *some* money left," repeated Cathy. "Even since father died we've been able to pay bills. There must be a little left; and if we have a sale and sell the furniture —"

"That *is* the point," explained Muriel. "Archy thinks that altogether there may be about a thousand pounds. But you know what bank-clerks earn to begin with! — and if Alan's to live in any really *nice* digs, of course he'll need a little extra. Archy thinks a thousand should just see him through till he gets a raise; whereas *you* won't need anything, because you're coming to live with us."

Again, Cathy had no alternative. Her very contempt for her brother's notion of independence made her too proud to stand on her rights; so she was penniless. She was also peculiarly unqualified to earn her own living, as Muriel, observing some hesitation on Cathy's part, pointed out. "You didn't even pass your Matric," reminded Muriel — though more, as the occasion demanded, in sorrow than in anger. "But I'm sure you can be the greatest help to us, especially with little Anna," she added kindly, "and Archy thinks so too — don't you, Archy?"

By this time they were back in the dining-room. Mr. Maclaren, brain-washed in advance, nodded coopera- tively. He even patted Cathy's hand. He felt none of Tommy Bamber's near-affection for a kid-sister, but having won such a pearl of a wife strung along with her.

"We're all going to be right as rain," encouraged Archy — patting Cathy's hand.

She looked across the table at Alan. Obviously much of what Muriel had been explaining to herself, about their meagre inheritance, Archy must have been ex- plaining to her brother. But Alan, insouciant as Mr. Pennon where money matters were concerned, appeared rather jolly . . .

What else could Cathy do but accept with what grati- tude she could summon (admittedly it wasn't much) a new home with the Maclarens?

16

EVERYTHING SHONE.
Not with the natural heat of the sun, but with furniture- and metal-polish. The furniture was polished, the floors were polished, the door-knocker was polished particularly. The table-silver was polished, the glasses were polished with glass-cloths and the mirrors with some special preparation for mirror-polishing. Muriel was a splendid housewife — so splendid in fact that she rarely kept a servant more than a month; and with great satisfaction saw the back of the last of them almost immediately upon Cathy's domestication. As Muriel said, it was quite a *small* house; also she genuinely felt that Cathy would be far more happy and contented, knowing she was of use.

To do Muriel justice, the sentiment projected on her sister would undoubtedly have been her own, their situations reversed. She always sought for good in people. "Now we shall really get the house looking nice!" promised Muriel joyfully; and when Cathy didn't exactly clap hands, invested her with the further appropriate emotion of daughterly grief.

"We must remember Cathy lived at home much longer than I did," said Muriel to Archy. "She was never demonstrative, but if you'd seen her face this morning, while we were washing paint, you'd have thought her quite heart-broken . . ."

The only item withdrawn by Muriel from the sale (at which the Benares brass trays fetched half-a-crown apiece, and the geishas little more) had been a parcel of table-linen. As she sensibly remarked, no one would pay much for it anyway, and it did contain several quite nice tea-table cloths edged with hand-made Island lace. — One of these had for further decoration, in the centre, a group of autographs over-embroidered in chain-stitch by Muriel herself: commemorating amongst others Henry Alistair McCrimmon (drowned in the North Sea), Henry Arthur Cooke (drowned in the Channel), and William Powell (blown up with his ship off Gallipoli).

"I must say I worked very neatly, even then," observed Muriel. "Whoever was Edward Collier?"

"Mother's Major," said Cathy. "He sang 'Tosti's Good-bye.'"

"What a memory you have! — Anyway, it's gone in the middle," said Muriel briskly. "We'll tear it up to wash paint."

Cathy, though she'd never much liked Major Collier, preserved the strip that bore his name as long as possible; but it frayed at last, to be thrown out with the other rags.

The Maclarens were as kind to Cathy as possible. She had her own room, with its own gas-fire, and her own subscription (Class B) to Boots' Library, and was also entrusted with sole charge of little Anna whenever Muriel and Archy went out together at night, as they were now able to do much more frequently. — Again to give

Muriel her due, she honestly believed Cathy must enjoy baby-sitting, because Anna was such a little love. It involved no mental effort at all to add to Cathy's character of disconsolate daughter that of devoted aunt.

"Who's going to be quite safe with Aunt Cathy?" cooed Muriel, bending over the cot with her hat on. "Baby Anna!"

2

"You little brute, you little beast, you little pest, go to sleep!" snarled Cathy.

The infant Anna, at four years old portly as a basset-pup, hair already promising to flame like her aunt's, deliberately rolled out of bed and stumped towards the window. "One of these days I'm going to skin you!" swore Cathy, catching her by the nightgown-tail — and for a moment stood herself transfixed. Beyond narrow back-gardens the hour-later, summer-time sun descended in such splendour, panes of green-houses glittered like rubies, even a sprinkler left on flung up diamonds, late-flowering laburnums tossed gold in the air; offering in all such an apocalyptic vision of suburbia as to astonish the oldest inhabitant and draw any child from bed.

"But you've never seen the sun on the Mediterranean," said Cathy contemptuously, turning her back. "You've never seen sun-pennies dancing on blue water . . ."

She man-handled Anna into her cot. Anna immediately rolled out again and created a new, less aesthetic diversion by grovelling under the wash-stand to produce a brown plush Teddy Bear.

"All right, have it in with you," said Cathy. "It's probably covered with germs . . ."

Even though she was Muriel's daughter, it could

hardly have been from a sense of hygiene that little Anna unexpectedly threw the toy out of the window. — Or rather, she didn't actually throw it; she waddled with it to the sill, sentimentally sat it up (as though to watch the sunset), then gave it a shove.

Cathy very nearly shoved Anna after. Fortunately some inhibition operated; Muriel and Archy returned to find their daughter with no bones broken.

"Did Aunt Cathy look after you nicely?" asked Muriel next morning — but purely as a matter of form. It wasn't to Muriel's surprise, it was to Cathy's, that little Anna nodded.

3

Muriel never put any such leading question to her husband, however, even during the brief early period while she was still, amongst envious friends, describing Cathy as really an answer to prayer. — All Muriel's friends, each with her own tale to tell of avaricious charwoman or incompetent daily, envied Muriel extremely. How much nicer, they cried, when one had to do half the work oneself anyway, to have the other half done by a sister, whom one could chat to and have jokes with! "Of course Mrs. Griffin still comes for the rough," reminded Muriel, "but I must say Cathy really *is* an answer to prayer!"

She for some time tried hard to believe it. But there was very little sisterly chat, as she and Cathy worked about the house together, and absolutely no cracking of jokes. To encourage her — or perhaps to encourage herself — "Who loves her Aunt Cathy?" cried Muriel gaily, often several times a day. But very soon the cry took on a rather nervous note. Muriel didn't know she had nerves, until Cathy got on them; while Archy's normal cheerfulness so diminished, she never dreamed of asking who loved his sister-in-law.

Archy, unlike Muriel, wasn't with Cathy all day, but he came home to her. He had been used to look forward above all things to coming home each night — not only to a well-cooked dinner but also to a smiling wife interested to hear everything he'd read in the evening paper. (Naturally he never brought gossip from the Bank, even when a cheque surprisingly bounced; he was far too correct a Bank Manager.) Now, though his meal was still well-cooked, Muriel could sometimes barely raise a smile; for another thing, Cathy regularly — out of boredom, or sheer cussedness? — nipped out to buy a paper herself and gave Muriel even the City headlines in advance. All freshness and surprise was gone, as Archy but repeated them; and though Muriel did her best to look astonished at, for example, a sensational drop in the Gold Reserve, Archy saw perfectly well that she knew about it already.

It was a small matter, but symptomatic. Yet how was it possible to forbid a sister-in-law's buying an evening paper? It wasn't possible. Indeed Cathy might well have retorted that on shillings a week pocket-money, it was about all she could buy at all.

Nor was it possible, given the circumstances of which this was one, to turn her out of doors and let her fend for herself. The bourgeois virtue of loyalty to one's kindred, in itself a very great virtue indeed, condemned Archy, Muriel and Cathy to a common discomfort with but one socially acceptable issue.

If only they could get Cathy married! The Maclarens often talked about it in bed at night. In bed was the only

94

time they could really talk at all, without the chance of Cathy overhearing.

"She has nice hair," mused Muriel, comfortably inserting her knees between Archy's. "When it's just been washed it's really pretty . . ."

"Ginger," said Archy.

"Chestnut," corrected Muriel. (She was already practising the euphemism on Anna's account.) "I only wish mine was . . ."

Archy Maclaren (to what surprise, had they been witnesses, of his colleagues at Barclays Bank) took a thick fair braid between his teeth and chewed it.

"Yours is honey-colour. You're honey-colour all over . . ."

"Darling, don't!" chided Muriel. "You know we ought to wait at least another year . . . Isn't there anyone you can bring home from the Bank?"

In fact Archy had brought several men home from the Bank. The Maclarens that autumn enjoyed quite a reputation, for hospitality. But there were two major difficulties. One was that the affections of a junior bank-clerk — all their elders, those capable of supporting a wife, were married already — notoriously involved a long engagement. The other difficulty was Cathy. Even in her mid-twenties, she hadn't ripened. On the contrary, after so many years' lack the deprivation of the sun showed in her limbs and features much as if she'd been as long deprived of food. She looked at once ferocious and half-starved . . .

"Any chap who tries to kiss her under this lot," observed Archy, as he hung the Christmas mistletoe, "will be a hero."

Muriel, remembering certain long-ago children's parties, sighed.

"And probably get his shins kicked into the bargain," added Archy — just as though he'd played Postman's Knock with his sister-in-law himself.

Muriel sighed again. It was dreadful to see Archy so cross on Christmas Eve, but she fully sympathized with his unfestive humour. She had already observed, as he happily dug out his Santa Claus outfit, Cathy's contemptuous glance. Archy Maclaren, early plump and rosy-complexioned, made a rather good Santa Claus; Muriel was accustomed to enjoy seeing him dress up as much as he enjoyed dressing up himself. Cathy's glance diminished both their pleasures — and Muriel could only hope no cat would be let out of the sack to diminish little Anna's too.

"Little Anna *believes* in Santa Claus," reminded Muriel.

"How idiotic," said Cathy.

"That's not a very nice way to talk at Christmas, dear. And I hope you don't mean you think Archy looks idiotic . . ."

It was an unwary assumption. Cathy's eye on her brother-in-law now preparing to tiptoe upstairs was bleaker than ever. He by this time wore the beard and whiskers Muriel preserved in tissue-paper all year, but hadn't removed a pair of rimless spectacles.

"If Anna's awake she'll recognize him and if she isn't what's the point?" enquired Cathy, with icy reason.

Of course there wasn't any point, except that Christmas is the time for dressing up, and being irrational and jolly, to console for the absence of the sun. Muriel and

Archy were better pagans than they knew, or than Cathy appreciated. That year however the festival was rather lack-lustre all round. Everything went awry. Alan, for example, invited to bring any friend he liked (perhaps bank-clerks came older, in the Midlands?) replied gratefully that her name was Alice, and when Muriel replied in turn that with only one spare room she was sorry but she obviously couldn't put up a girl, Alan didn't come either. All Archy's bachelor colleagues for some reason or other equally absconded, and in the end only the Maclarens and Cathy sat down to an over-size turkey they'd have to go on eating all week. Afterwards they pulled crackers and put caps on their heads. Cathy drew the piratical sort with a skull-and-cross-bones in front. It was rather a relief when she immediately withdrew upstairs with a Class B novel, leaving Archy and Muriel to play tiddlywinks with little Anna.

"Count me out at Hogmanay," said Mr. Maclaren. "I'll be spending it with the London Scottish."

He was as good as his word. At dawn on New Year's Day Muriel for the first time in their married life had to take her husband's boots off for him.

She still, as always, did her best. Miss Allen would have been proud of her. However concerned for Archy gulping black coffee in a hot bath — however concerned, more broadly, for their whole domestic future — Muriel still felt truly if uncomprehendingly concerned for her sister; and as she couldn't find Cathy a husband, suggested a course in dressmaking offered by the London County Council at their institute in the Charing Cross Road.

Which would at least take Cathy out of the house two days a week.

97

"Just think, you'll be able to make smocks for little Anna!" encouraged Muriel.

She couldn't visualize Cathy getting much further, nor indeed could Cathy; who still enrolled willingly enough, to get out of the house twice a week.

4

Cathy in fact disliked the L.C.C. dressmaking-school almost as much as she'd disliked Miss Allen's. The best of her fellow-students resembled Muriel and the worst Judith Bamber. Only a male teacher of Design, lanky and black-haired, aroused her least interest, and him she never encountered save occasionally in a corridor — being literally out of his class.

But the Charing Cross Road marches with Soho. Cathy, discovering a street of small shops where coarse bread was sold and garlic hung in strings, even in January loitered there at the day's end and was sometimes late home; once especially so. — Separating the shops were certain narrow anonymous doors, often ajar; alongside one, idly surveying the passing scene, leant a dark, stocky young man of striking appearance. He wore a splendid camel-hair coat, bright yellow shoes and flashy shirt: above the collar of which, incongruously beautiful, reared the head of a bronze faun.

17

"JACKO!" CRIED CATHY.

They had sat opposite each other over their poker-hands, each scrutinizing the other's face for a least betraying change of expression, too often for recognition not to be mutual.

"Well, I'm dashed," said Jacko. "Been drawing to any broken straights?"

Cathy shook her rough red head.

"I haven't had the chance. Besides, didn't I promise?"

"That's right," recalled Jacko. "Still, you look as if you had."

His manner had greatly increased in self-confidence, from the Next-door Island days. It wasn't exactly familiar; it was part of his general aplomb. Cathy noticed that he wore also a large gold wrist-watch and a large gold ring.

"*You* look splendid," she said admiringly. "Oh, Jacko, I can't tell you how glad I am to see you again! But weren't you going to be a steward on the P. and O.? What are you doing at Home?"

Before he could answer, at that moment there emerged from the doorway behind him a young woman of astonishing beauty. Cathy had never seen such vivid colouring;

even shadowed between a high fox-fur collar and a deep cloche hat, her ruby lips and rosy cheeks made immediate impact. She gave Jacko a casual nod; he nodded back and glanced at his watch.

"Is she an actress?" asked Cathy, momentarily diverted.

"In a way," said Jacko. "Look, you didn't ought to be talking to me —"

"Nonsense," said Cathy. "Didn't I talk to you even on the Island? Didn't you teach me to play poker?" She paused an instant; she had so much to say, so many questions to ask, she didn't know where to begin. "Oh, Jacko, do you remember the Governor?"

"Certainly I do," said Jacko, diverted in turn. "He didn't give the order to fire."

"*What?*"

"In India, or somewhere, while he was still Army, he didn't give the order to fire. So fifty dead in a riot. Didn't you know? All the Island did," said Jacko. "That's why he was Governor — kicked up out of harm, as my dad said. Of course you were young."

"I wasn't too young to know he was wonderful," said Cathy hotly. "If he didn't fire, he was quite right."

"Retired early all the same," pointed out Jacko knowledgeably. "Kicked six storeys up."

"Then you've seen him too?" cried Cathy.

"Certainly I have," said Jacko. "Every time I met a boat-train I used to see him, perched up on that balcony like a stuffed hawk. — The new one seems a bit of a terror," added Jacko, "at least his wife is, Mum writes: she's had half Government House hangings taken down and moth-balled."

It was wonderful to be hearing Island-talk again; just

then, however, there emerged from the doorway a second remarkable beauty, this time blonde and bare-headed. She too gave Jacko a nod; again, with an air of returning to duty — rather with the air of a traffic-inspector clocking vehicles past a control-point — he glanced at his watch.

"Is she another?" asked Cathy interestedly.

"That's right," said Jacko. "Look, I'm sorry not to ask you in —"

It was a mistake, but he spoke without thinking. Cathy seized the implication in a flash.

"You mean you live here? But that's wonderful! It's quite close to my dressmaking! If there's a poker-school —"

"There's not," said Jacko hastily.

"Well, let's start one," urged Cathy. "I can easily cut afternoons. It would only be twice a week —"

But Jacko stood pat.

"Strictly no gambling allowed. Too much of a distraction. Look, it's been nice seeing you —"

"But you haven't told me yet what you're doing!" protested Cathy, clutching at his sleeve as he backed through the door. "What *are* you doing, Jacko?"

Under her urgent gaze he made a clean breast of it.

"If you must know, I run a theatrical boarding-house. — All right, so I could've skipped ship at Marseilles," said Jacko defensively. "By now I could have been a croupier at Monte. I could easily've found someone —" here his hand involuntarily sketched in the air a ripe female form — "to put up a bond for me. But it would've meant taking out papers, and I was too proud of my British nationality."

Cathy had always liked Jacko. His loyalty to the Raj

made her like him even more, and she promised herself many another delightful conversation when he was less pressed for time. — Indeed, she felt revivified already, and if, as has been said, got home late, for once looked so much brighter, so almost cheerful, Muriel didn't scold.

"I believe Cathy's really going to *enjoy* dressmaking," murmured Muriel that night. "And just think, if she gets any good at it she'll be able to make things for me too . . ."

"All *I* can see your sister ever making," responded Archy drowsily, "is a hair shirt."

"Don't be silly, darling."

" 'Stitch, stitch, stitch in poverty hunger and pain.' "

"Don't be silly," repeated Muriel, turning over, "they have the most lovely materials at Harrods."

So rapidly did a touch of the sun work on Cathy, between the Thursday when she'd encountered Jacko and the Tuesday of her next class the tension in the house perceptibly relaxed. For one thing (her mind busy marshalling the many more questions she wanted to put to Jacko) she forgot to buy an evening paper; Muriel was genuinely astonished to hear that Domestic Appliances had passed a dividend. Her mind, despite Jacko's stubbornness, busy exploring the possibilities of a new poker-school, Cathy taught little Anna to play Beggar-My-Neighbour. Anna loved playing Beggar-My-Neighbour, if only because all children love playing any game with an adult who takes it seriously, and Cathy took at least the dealing part seriously. She was less out of practice than she feared; over a nursery table the cards soon streamed as smoothly from her hands as in a bathing-box on the Next-door Island.

2

"What, you again?" said Jacko.

— The brunette, at that moment clocking out, for a joke threw Cathy a friendly smile. (To his credit, Jacko was a bully only in the technical sense.) Cathy smiled gratefully in return, and asked Jacko what play she was in. "*Macbeth*," said Jacko. (Anyone who had any English education at all on the Next-door Island knew Macbeth.) "One of the three witches," added Jacko, slightly raising his voice. (The back of the fox-fur collar wiggled appreciatively.) "Now look, didn't I say before you didn't ought to be speaking to me?"

"And didn't *I* say it was nonsense?" retorted Cathy. "Don't be silly and tell me what's happened to the Governor. You said you *used* to see him —"

"Not any more," agreed Jacko — glancing at his wristwatch, but perhaps not himself unhappy to fall into Island-talk again. "Take a dekko at that balcony now, all you'll see's an old bid watering geraniums. But as to where he's packed up to I was by some oversight not informed. — I'll tell you another thing you didn't know about the Governor," added Jacko, with a sudden grin, "he had a key to a house on Strada San Giorgio."

"I saw a photograph in his flat," recalled Cathy interestedly, "but I didn't know he had a house."

"All the Island did," grinned Jacko. "As I say, you were young. Now look, dear, since there's strictly no poker going —"

"Why not?" murmured the bare-headed blonde, at that moment emerging in turn. "It'd make a nice change, and you could take the same rake-off . . ."

"Then that's three of us," said Cathy eagerly. "And if your friend — ?"

"Olive," supplied the blonde. "I'm Sylvia. And we're both *mad* on poker."

"For goodness' sake, Jacko, can't you find a fifth?" adjured Cathy. "It's nonsense to call poker gambling, you've told me yourself it's a game of skill. Actually the man who teaches dress-design — at the L.C.C.," she threw in, to Sylvia, "looks a bit like a poker-player. Should I ask him?"

Jacko, for all his aplomb, under his lodger's malicious eye needed to brace himself against the door-jamb.

"Look," begged Jacko, "if you'll run along now, I'll think about it . . ."

Behind him as he hastily retreated Cathy glimpsed a small dark room hung with religious pictures; sniffed garlic; already in fancy munched a slice of coarse dark bread smeared with oil.

3

"If you're often going to be late," said Muriel, but quite amiably, "I'd better keep you something hot."

"Yes, I dare say I am," agreed Cathy, "if it isn't a nuisance."

It was practically her first civil utterance under the Maclaren roof.

"If you'd like," suggested Muriel, "as you're getting on so well, to go *three* days a week, I'm sure little Anna and I could manage . . ."

For literally the first time under the Maclaren roof Cathy looked grateful. — Half the virtue of a good poker-school derives from regularity, frequency, and the resultant familiarity: scratch made-up games when

104

it takes half a session to learn who bluffs and whom to see offer little more than gambling indeed. Cathy fancied Sylvia a bluffer and Olive more dangerous; Jacko's classic game she knew by heart; their fifth, whether the man from the L.C.C. or someone produced by Jacko, was unnecessarily an unknown quantity; but if they could all play together three times a week, Cathy felt assured of a true game of skill.

Joyfully she hastened to quench Jacko's last doubts. — It was raining a little, but not because of the rain Cathy almost ran, towards that narrow anonymous door. She in fact didn't notice the rain, dampening and darkening and sleeking her bare hair from rough ginger to smooth chestnut, nor the several wolf-whistles excited in consequence. A death's-head under the mistletoe, Cathy streaking through rain to set up a poker-school looked so almost attractive, Muriel seeing her would have taken fresh heart.

Unfortunately Jacko wasn't there. Also the door was shut. Cathy knocked but got no answer. Nor was Jacko there the next week, nor the week after. As a British national he couldn't be deported; but he could be jailed.

18

IN AGAIN, OUT again, such was Jacko's life. He accepted it, he made his dispositions, and his lodgers were faithful. Like a couple of Bournemouth dowagers switching from their favourite Seaview to Chinedown only while Seaview is being redecorated, if Olive and Sylvia necessarily switched digs while he was in, it was always on the understanding that they should switch back when he came out.

Why not? Jacko possessed virtues which would have been virtues in any stratum of society. He was for example a strict teetotaller; also very pious; not a Sunday passed but he lit a candle in St. Patrick's Soho Square with an intention to his mother. He was economical, businesslike, and self-educated in several minor branches of both medicine and law. An added virtue in his own milieu was the reputation of having rough friends. Jacko himself was never involved in what is technically known as an affray, he was far too well-conducted; it just so happened that any rival landlord making trouble for one of his lodgers, or any guest of that lodger demanding more, so to speak, than was on the menu, not uncommonly found one of Jacko's loyal, rough friends standing by. Naturally Sylvia and Olive appreciated this attention to their interests very much — just as a couple of Bourne-mouth dowagers might appreciate the manager of Sea-view's attention to their respective diets — and were always glad to welcome Jacko back.

"Olive and me kept an eye on things as well as we could," reported Sylvia, some six months later. "We don't think the water's been cut off, nor the gas. But of course there's been no laundry sent."

Jacko as usual on his return from a spell inside took a housekeeperly dekko at the linen and reached for the telephone (fortunately not cut off either) to alert the Quaker Maid Laundry. Sylvia and Olive exchanged happy looks. They were as strong on hygiene as Jacko himself — at the moment smelling strongly of carbolic soap.

19

IT WAS MEANWHILE a great disappointment to Muriel that Cathy seemed to have lost all interest in dressmaking: Lent term ended fruitless of even a smock for little Anna. Muriel suggested a course in pottery; Cathy wasn't interested in pottery either. Nor was she interested in batik, poster-design or weaving. She could still have enrolled and then cut classes; there was all London to explore, far beyond the confines of Soho; but even during the last weeks of dressmaking she had had enough of wandering about London alone. She re-treated, like an animal into its narrow but familiar bur-row — in this case a room with a gas-fire and a Class B subscription to Boots'.

At this period, in fact, Cathy was reading novels much as Mrs. Pennon had done, swallowing down one after the other with a sort of idle appetite; Mrs. Pennon's literary sheet-anchor had been Rider Haggard, Cathy's was Joseph Conrad; otherwise they were equally omnivor-ous — and idle. Muriel and Mrs. Griffin did the spring-cleaning between them, little Anna pulled a pack of cards about unheeded, while Cathy read novel after novel and sent the gas-bills up. In a way this new addiction made her easier to live with, but Muriel felt it unhealthy, especially as the spring afternoons lengthened and Cathy, unlike even the timid coney and blind mole, still showed no disposition to stir abroad.

Conscientious as ever —

"Why not come to Harrods with me?" suggested Muriel, opening Cathy's door and receiving full in the face a buffet of over-heated air.

But Cathy shook a bemused, sulky head, and Muriel went to Harrods alone.

2

Muriel loved going to Harrods. It was her great aesthetic pleasure to linger between the beautifully set-out counters, breathing the bright warm air, treading the soft clean carpets. To Muriel it was like being in some great glorious conservatory, with for a display of orchids a case of costume-jewellery, instead of gardenias Swiss handkerchieves abloom; silks and brocades drooped from their stands like glossy-leaved, exotic-fruited vines. There were also the odours: actually of violet and sweet-geranium, in the soap department, but even these scarcely less heady than the emanations from the new, unlaundered Household Furnishings on the floors above. Muriel emerging from the lift, pausing by a pile of friction-towels, smelled fresh-cut hay . . .

What she had in fact come for was a pair of pillow-slips. She never bought more than two at a time, and would have preferred to buy one by one, so as to have additional occasions for Harrodizing, only pillow-slips were as inevitably paired as kippers. Thus she was in no hurry to be served, but waited in complete patience while a customer ahead at the linen-counter had her order checked. — The size of this was interesting in itself, particularly when the customer (a small nondescript woman in a mackintosh) casually added, to twenty pairs of double-sheets and thirty of single, a couple of dozen bolster-cases. "Napkins?" suggested the assistant — loyally summoning, by a glance, his colleague from across the aisle; but it appeared that six dozen (best damask) were already ordered, together with four of best Irish-linen glass-cloths. In fact quite a coterie of happy assistants gathered, to check a final list which included, besides, ten pair of Witney blankets: five dozen yellow dusters: ditto checked ditto; and six friction-towels.

"A' to be sent, of course, to Strathspey," said Miss McCorquodale.

For Corky it was. Muriel, alerted by that familiar voice, and turning for a fuller look, recognized her at once. Corky was but a little greyer, a little bonier; otherwise unchanged. Glad as Cathy re-encountering Jacko —

"Miss McCorquodale!" cried Muriel.

3

"That's right," agreed Miss McCorquodale amiably — also as one used to being addressed in Harrods. "Just doing a wee bit of shopping for the Castle . . ."

She hadn't been romancing after all, on the Next-door Island; and hurrying home under the threat of war, forced at last to claim that second-cousinship, had been installed by the dear Duke as housekeeper at Strathspey. — Muriel, with her specialized social intelligence, from the single word "castle" accurately deduced the whole situation. It made her gladder than ever to claim acquaintance.

"I'm Muriel Pennon — that is, Muriel Maclaren," she explained eagerly. "I wonder if you remember me?"

"Indeed I do," said Corky, who by now had had time for a reciprocal scrutiny. "I remember you pairfectly: ten for conduct, and damn little for aught else." (She *had* changed. It was remarkable how renewed contact with her native heath, or perhaps with the dear Duke, had promoted her self-confidence; she used a damn as to the manner born.) "Still, if you're married, that was all could be hoped," added Miss McCorquodale kindly. "How're your wee brother and sister faring?"

"Well, Alan's in my husband's Bank —" began Muriel.

"Learnt his twice times in a jiffy," agreed Miss McCorquodale. "And Cathy?"

Muriel sighed; then remembering what sad news she had to break sighed again, more importantly.

"Since we lost both our parents, a year ago —"

"Dearie me! Did they hold out as long as that?" said Miss McCorquodale. "Megrims and weak chest and a'?"

"— Cathy's been living with *us*."

"Poor souls!" said Miss McCorquodale — but whether in reference to Mr. and Mrs. Pennon, or to Muriel and her husband, or possibly including Cathy, was difficult to tell, especially as she at the same moment (as it were in parenthesis) brushed off an assistant trailing a lace banquet-cloth. Muriel however had no intention of letting her, and Archy's, benevolence be brushed off too. She sighed again.

"And Cathy's not exactly . . . easy, you know. She never was."

"You should do something for that asthma," said

Miss McCorquodale. "Cannot she earn any living of her own? I admit her marks always shaky —"

"*Here*, she didn't even pass Matric.," confessed Muriel, "and we can hardly let her go as a shop-assistant." (It was actually the presence of a half-a-dozen shop-assistants standing round that suggested the phrase. However, since the Castle subsequently found itself dowered with a superfluous banquet-cloth, one assistant at least couldn't complain.) "Archy — my husband — has been simply wonderful," went on Muriel. "Really a saint! And when you think we've a little daughter —"

She paused, giving Miss McCorquodale an opening for either sympathy or congratulation. The latter however chose rather a middle course.

"Just stick to your duty and it's been verra nice seeing you," said Miss McCorquodale. "Now, since Groceries ca' —"

"How I wish you could see little Anna!" interposed Muriel. "Look, here's my card; perhaps next time you're in Town — ?"

"Dear knows when *that*'ll be," said Miss McCorquodale.

Muriel made up her mind in a flash. — It had to be in a flash because Corky was already moving off. There was just time to remember an uncut cake at home, and how sweet Anna looked in her bath, and that Archy, if Miss McCorquodale could be detained long enough, would probably enjoy hearing about Strathspey just as much as she herself would . . .

"Or won't you come back with me now?" pressed Muriel. "My husband would be so glad to meet you! Won't you come back to tea with me now?"

But times had changed, from the Next-door Island

days when Corky received an invitation to tea no more than once a month, and then on sufffrance. Slightly lifting and wagging her umbrella —

"For dear's sake," exclaimed Miss McCorquodale, "if there isn't Lady Maud — and Mrs. Anstruther wi' her! 'Twas always said to be the Long Bar at Singapore for meeting old friends — but give *me* Harrods!"

4

"Whoever do you think I met in Harrods?" cried Muriel, hardly waiting to take her hat off. "Corky! And it was all perfectly true!"

Indeed Miss McCorquodale, probably alone among the returning Islanders, had found every promise of Home fulfilled.

20

WHATEVER ALAN'S EXPECTATIONS had been, he too was well satisfied with his present condition. Alan, in the Midlands, was in clover.

The work at the Bank came easily to him; in his digs the promised motherly landlady spoiled him as he hadn't been spoiled since the days of Carmela. He was given a cup of tea before he got up, then an enormous breakfast, then an equally enormous high-tea as soon as he returned in the evening. He filled out. He also reverted to character as Don Juan of the Upper First.

There are very pretty girls in the Midlands. Some were actually typists employed in the same Bank. But with a discretion that would have pleased his brother-in-law Alan kept his amours extra-mural — culling here a blossom from Woolworth's (his old stamping-ground), there a bud (Alice) from the newer pastures of the Co-operative Stores. Again to his credit, he actually fertilized neither, but lost his virginity in the arms of whom but his own landlady.

He was fortunate. Sweetly, smoothly, in a thoroughly comfortable brass bed, a big bosom welcomed; sweetly, smoothly, the big thighs parted, and Alan plunged as into sun-warmed waters.

Everything sparkled. A flicker of low gas-light on the frame of the text above the bed transmuted gilt to pure gold. (Thou Lord Seest Me: the capitals also gilded, also sparkling.) A hair-pin on the pillow gleamed like the spine of an angel's feather; the brass knobs and curlicues seemed to throw off particles of light. Alan, plunging again and again, at last remembered sun-pennies . . .

"Now be still, thou little imp!" chided his landlady, tenderly. "Be still and go to sleep!"

21

THE SUBSEQUENT LETTER from Miss Mc-
Corquodale, rather to Muriel's dissatisfaction, was
addressed directly to Cathy; its contents however were
such that she not only swallowed the affront but found
its after-taste luscious. For why Corky wrote was to offer
her ex-pupil the chance to apply for the post of nursery-
governess with Lady Jean (His Grace's youngest), now
married in Devon and mother of a seven-year-old daughter.

"Devon!" cried Muriel enthusiastically. "How lovely!
Why, it's the garden of England!"

"Kent," said Cathy.

"Kent?" repeated Muriel — a little put out of her
stride.

"The garden of England. If *you* didn't learn it, at that
school we went to, I did," said Cathy. "It's Kent that's
the garden of England."

"Anyway, I'm sure you'd love it," said Muriel hastily.
"And you're so good with small children! I can't think
what little Anna's going to do without you!"

"If I'm hired," said Cathy. "That is, if I apply."

She spoke nonetheless, as she at that time so often and
so ungratefully spoke, simply to be disagreeable: in fact

any employment that changed her condition would have found Cathy ready and willing. — Muriel, who naturally had no idea of this, went on persuading.

"Not to be snobbish, dear, it *is* with Lady Jean. I mean, Archy and I couldn't possibly let you go just *anywhere*. It's what Corky must have realized —"

"What did you tell her about me?" asked Cathy suspiciously.

"Why, just that you were living with us," said Muriel.

"Good old Corky."

"And how thoughtful she's been!" continued Muriel — who had inherited something of her mother's deaf ear when necessary. "She's even arranged for Lady Jean to pay your railway fare!"

"You'll have to give it me first," said Cathy pointedly.

The Maclarens were so happy to do so, they dispatched Cathy first-class; and only too late realized that a nursery-governess travelling First might create a wrong impression. However the ticket (on Cathy's insistence a return) had been bought and paid for by Archy in advance; so first-class Cathy went.

Sullenly all the same she settled into her comfortable seat. She had no sense of adventure, of embarking upon a new life; she was simply getting away from the Maclarens. Sullenly she closed her eyes to the passing, increasingly pastoral landscape; and only on descending at Wellscombe Halt discovered that the England of her childish picture-books existed after all.

Part Three

22

WHOEVER DESIGNED THE first small rural
stations of a nation in the grip of the railway-
mania had obviously kept his head and possibly spent
his holidays in Switzerland. Faced by the need to bait,
if not actually stable, an iron horse, this unknown stal-
wart sensibly decided to domesticate it. Not for him
the Roman grandeur of Euston whence roared ex-
presses to the far North; lesser, humbler engines loiter-
ing along branch-lines were at every halt reminded of
their forerunners — stage-coach, or even pack-horse —
by a certain bucolic simplicity in the lay-out of ticket-
office, waiting-room, and shed for lamps. The Swiss
gingerbread eaves but fantasticated a wayside inn; and
whether there were two benches on the platform or only
one, there was always space for a garden.

The railway-servants of a nation in the grip of the
railway-mania in fact gardened with such passion, it became one of their recognized functions, with prizes to be
gained, or at least certificates for framing. Wellscombe
Halt had actually achieved a First three years running,
and in June looked less like a railway-station than a
pergola. Besides roses, clematis particularly flourished,
showing in purple and white from the solitary lamp-post;

honeysuckle and jasmine swarmed a rough rural trellis murmurous with bees. From a cranny in the gingerbread a dove fluttered out, and through the gate at the level-crossing peeped a little pinafored girl . . .

Cathy was still gazing astounded when a chauffeur in livery approached and asked her name. Bemusedly she gave it; and during the short drive to Wellscombe Manor could only look out at, and wonder at, more flowers in the hedgerows than she knew the names of. The high summer sun burnished a buttercup-field beyond to a sheet of cloth-of-gold, a clump of dandelions to a rosette of gold lace. Everything sparkled, from the buttons on the chauffeur's livery to the vane on a tree-embosomed steeple, from the underside of a willow-leaf to the brass knob on a cottage door. Upon the west windows of Wells-combe Manor the sun so beat, striped blinds had been lowered; the comparative cool within but reminded of the sun's power. — Only one room remained unshaded: a small parlour in which Lady Jean (a sun-lover herself) waited to interview Corky's latest find.

2

There is a type of English beauty — blue-eyed, fair-haired, slender-limbed and translucently complexioned — that approximates more nearly to a Botticelli than anything to be found in the Italy of to-day. Such beauty was Lady Jean's. Cathy had not only discovered Birket Foster's England, she had rediscovered the Madonna.

Like the Madonna's, Lady Jean's mouth curved in a sweet, tolerant smile that blessed even the dustiest here-tic — in this case, a potential nursery-governess.

"Miss Pennon? First of all sit down and have tea," said Lady Jean. "— Or perhaps not; perhaps first of all you'd better see the horrid child you're desperate enough to want to take charge of."

"How did you know I was desperate?" asked Cathy. It seemed like a miracle. But before the Madonna could answer a cherub materialized at her knee; equally ethereal in blue-eyed, fair-haired translucence, but dimpled.

"She must have been hiding," apologized Lady Jean. "Elspet, say good afternoon to Miss Pennon! — She won't," added Lady Jean helplessly. "She's in one of her shy fits. Do you think you could *stand* her?"

Cathy nodded dumbly. She put out her hand, waiting as stilly as for a butterfly to settle. — There was nothing awkward about the child's shyness; for a seven-year-old she was remarkably composed; solemn, as it were gracious, only mute. For a moment she considered Cathy with grave attention; then lightly, like a butterfly, touched the proffered hand with her own and flitted from the room.

"But she's a little love . . ." murmured Cathy — or was it Muriel?

"Yes, isn't she?" said Lady Jean. "And thank Heavens she's taken to you. Now tea!"

Tea was brought in by a butler. Besides hot scones there were cucumber sandwiches and rolls of thin bread-and-butter; there was also fruit-cake. Cathy, whom Muriel had provided with a rather light lunch, felt almost ashamed of her appetite as Lady Jean but sipped a cup of China tea; but such was the Madonna's sweet tolerance, had barely a mouthful left to swallow on the way upstairs.

"To inspect your quarters!" smiled Lady Jean.

The huge nursery-schoolroom (west-facing, sun-

123

flooded) was by comparison with the rest of the house modern; situated in the upper reaches of a Victorian wing. It still appeared to Cathy like a schoolroom in a story-book. Between a dolls'-house and a rocking-horse reared a papier-mâché fort improbably manned by Life Guards; the coloured prints on the walls were *Cherry Ripe* and *When Did You Last See Your Father*, the *Infant Samuel* by Reynolds and *Cat's Christmas* by Louis Wain. A couple of low shelves housed almost complete sets of Henty and Rider Haggard — "I'm sure you're a great book-worm!" cried Lady Jean — and several bound volumes of the *Illustrated London News*. The small bedroom designated to a governess, adjoining, was papered with an original Morris pattern of grapes and pomegranates that didn't clash with, rather genially accepted, a quilt of eighteenth-century patchwork . . .

"Could you *bear* it?" implored Lady Jean, wafting Cathy downstairs again. "And Elspet too?"

"If you'll have me," said Cathy groggily.

"Then it's really yes? You really are an answer to prayer?" As light-fingered as her daughter, but more impulsive, Lady Jean brushed not Cathy's hand but her cheek in a swift gesture of gratitude. Then she sighed. "Oh, dear," sighed Lady Jean, "I suppose now we've got to talk about *money!* Which I must say is something I hate doing with anyone I like. I didn't in the least mind discussing money with Nanny Scott — who was such a tremendously qualified nursery-nurse she quite terrorized me. *You* wouldn't terrorize me?" asked Lady Jean anxiously.

Cathy, watching a low ray of sun light the exquisite features of the Madonna, could only smile.

"I don't believe you would," agreed Lady Jean. "You're too nice. Besides," she added humorously, "being quite *un*qualified! — for Corky tells me you didn't even pass Matric. Now, shall I conceal that from my husband or shan't I? After all, Elspet's just a mite . . ."

"I've taught my niece," said Cathy quickly. (It pricked her conscience to recall, only Beggar-My-Neighbour, but there are some situations in which deceit may surely be excused.) "I'm sure I could teach her anyway for a year or two . . ."

"Oh, so am I!" agreed Lady Jean. "But the awful thing is," she meditated agitatedly, "I *like* you. My husband's going to spot it at once, as soon as I talk to him; and then *he*'ll start arguing about Matriculation, and say I'm just going on a hunch. Oh dear," sighed Lady Jean, "look at us both now, when five minutes ago we were so happy together! How I wish you could come to us just as a *friend* — with pocket-money, of course: say fifteen shillings a week."

Beglamoured as she was, Cathy hesitated. She knew very little about money, or the rate for the job; a salary of some thirty pounds per annum still struck her as low. — Of course to Lady Jean it wasn't a salary at all, just pocket-money for friend; Cathy, whose Pennon grandfather had pulled himself up by his boot-straps, nonetheless hesitated.

"Of course there'd be travel as well," threw in Lady Jean. "This winter, for instance, Elspet and I set out on a little jaunt to Malta. Should you *mind* coming to Malta?"

It was another miracle.

It was such a miracle, Cathy forgot every other consideration. She had to speak almost gruffly, for fear of bursting into tears.

"As a matter of fact, I was brought up on the Next-door Island . . ."

"You were?" exclaimed Lady Jean delightedly. — "But of course," she recollected, "Corky said so. So you'd know all about it, and never let Elspet drink goat's milk and get Malta fever?"

"There hasn't been Malta fever for years," said Cathy loyally. "But I know about mosquito-bites."

"Then you really will come to us?" begged Lady Jean. "Just, as I've said, as a friend?"

Of course Cathy surrendered. For the sake of returning to the sun, however temporarily, she'd have taken ten pounds a year, or five, or nothing; and if at the back of her mind there lurked some idea of skipping ship, wasn't the immediate prospect of living at the Manor just as a friend as dazzling as sun-pennies?

So Cathy was hired. She telephoned the happy news to Muriel that same evening, so that Muriel could send her box; as Lady Jean pointed out, it was absurd to go to the expense of a fresh double journey when one of the housemaids could easily lend a nightie. "And remember *I* pay your fare down!" said Lady Jean. "I owe you twenty-five and twopence!" — Actually it was four pounds three and ten, Cathy having travelled First, and having made Archy take a return; but she couldn't very well say so.

23

NATURALLY THE NEWS got back to Harrods. Meeting a friend at the linen-counter during the summer sales —

"I hear dear Jean has a new attendant sprite," said Lady Jean's aunt Lady Maud. "Why can't you and I find attendant sprites?"

"Because we're too old and too fat and too ugly," said Mrs. Anstruther. "My dear, when you consider what Jean's sheer *looks* have done for her — !"

"Certainly she nobbled Lutterel on 'em," agreed Lady Maud. "My poor brother couldn't give her a ha'penny. — What are *you* after?"

"Napkins," said Mrs. Anstruther. "But only if they're really reduced."

"As nothing one wants ever *is*," sighed Lady Maud. — "Now we've missed our turn to that hussy with the Eton crop."

Times were changing, even at Harrods. The assistant behind the counter (not Corky's, quite young), knew perfectly well who the two old trouts were; and that their charge-accounts dated from Doomsday, and that their cheques never bounced; he still passed them up in favour of mascara'd eyelashes and a blonde Eton crop.

This was actually the first time Cathy was given her rightful, inherited title. All young women at Wellscombe started off as nannies or nursery-governesses, and all ended up as attendant sprites.

24

LADY JEAN WAS Lady Jean Lutterel. She hadn't actually married beneath her: Lutterels on their own ground outfaced in pride of lineage any one of James the First's casually created dukedoms, and that of Strathspey dated but from 1604. The earliest Lutterel family portraits were to be found not in the Manor's long gallery, but on the walls of Wellscombe church, as donors of, and immortalized in, a peculiarly realistic fresco of hell. It quite fascinated Cathy, sitting in the front pew, to observe how accurately down the centuries had been transmitted Mr. Lutterel's ugly long nose and short upper lip; the brasses underfoot but added a flowing moustache — in turn to be reproduced, after a gap of some six hundred years, in Lady Jean's favourite photograph of a nephew in the R.A.F. It appeared that the Lutterels, disdaining to be ennobled, simply strung along with English history even to its most minor details.

So did the ancient Lutterel dwelling string along. Its heart was the great hall, built over and around for six centuries; a panel of glass let into Tudor wainscotting showed behind it wattle-and-daub; the hearth at one end, now a handsome affair of white marble (spoil of some Lutterel returning from the Grand Tour) had perhaps once been located in the centre to let out smoke through a hole in the roof; still under the Renaissance cherubim a fire burned all the year round. A Bible-box, its oaken lid carved with Adam and Eve, dated from Oliver Cromwell; turned to secular use, to hold gloves and dog-leashes, it nonetheless retained a certain *mana*; gloves and leashes were never to be left lying upon it, they had to be placed, superstitiously, within. This Bible-box stood on a table just inside the great door, and was the first thing one saw on entering. The next thing one saw, across a stretch of marble flags and a Turkey rug, was a grandfather clock made for the Great Exhibition of 1851. It was quite peculiarly ugly, combining the silhouette of a gothic tower with a triple dial telling the time in London, St. Petersburg, and (a final *jeu d'esprit*) Constantinople.

Cathy liked the hall very much. It reminded her of the Governor's on the Next-door Island. The staircase rose in the same way, centrally, to a wide landing where if there were no men-at-arms there were tapestries — depicting not martyrdoms, however, but *fêtes champêtres*: on one side of a long dim mirror hung Spring, on the other Summer. Cathy on her way upstairs often paused several moments between them, looking down at the hall and liking it.

So did she sometimes see Mr. Lutterel pause and look, across towards the great door. It was still the front door to the house, locked at night by a huge iron key which to his wife's amusement and his tailor's despair Mr. Lutterel kept in a pocket. Compared with the rest of his accoutrements — slender cigarette-case, slim watch and slimmer watch-chain — the big iron key was a clashing burden; Mr. Lutterel nonetheless persisted in loading himself with it.

He was considerably older than his wife; the sitting Tory member for the constituency, and a hard-working one. While the House was in session Wellscombe saw little of him except at week-ends.

2

Lady Jean, besides looking like a Botticelli, was a very good sitting member's wife. On the high non-party plane vice-president of the International Friendship League (designed to heal the wounds of war by having foreigners to tea), she also opened and attended bazaars right and left. — This no mere turn of phrase; naturally all local Conservative bazaars were opened by Lady Jean, but she also attended all the Labour ones. Labour couldn't stop her, though its prospective candidate for the next election (a Mr. Hughes, ex–London School of Economics) would have liked to. Even when it was pointed out to her that the purchase of a mere lavender-bag actually contributed to Opposition funds, Lady Jean sweetly replied that she still knew who'd *made* the lavender-bags — nice Miss Palmer at the Post Office — and that Miss Palmer would like her to buy one. This was alas all too true; Mr. Hughes couldn't deny it; and continued to be embarrassed by a graceful presence drifting in his wake wearing a picture hat. — "Shades of Gainsborough, dear God!" murmured Lady Jean, thrusting in the long pins. Her hat never blew off, as once, at an open air fête did Mrs. Hughes's. Lady Jean could waltz in a tiara — also secured by long pins. She was particularly admired for giving up the London Season to stay and work in the constituency as her husband worked for it at Westminster.

"Her ladyship's had more Seasons than she can count," said Mr. Hughes sharply, when Miss Palmer drew his attention to this point. He was irritated at having been led to talk about the Season at all; also the term "her ladyship," by intention fraught with irony, he perceived Miss Palmer to find simply natural. "Jean Lutterel," Mr. Hughes corrected himself, "is probably as bored by a London Season as you are by a Mothers' Meeting."

"I'm sure *I* shouldn't be bored at a Mothers' Meeting at all," said Miss Palmer, slightly flushing. "And I still maintain, Mr. Hughes, that it shows a great sense of duty, and responsibility, which I only hope our own leaders will emulate. — How lovely she must look," added Miss Palmer, on a softer note, "waltzing in a tiara!"

Mr. Hughes was happy to think that there was absolutely no Labour festivity at which Lady Jean could appear with a tiara on her head; otherwise he simply had to give her best.

3

Of course the Lutterels were very poor — the "new poor," as Lady Jean wryly lamented, in contradistinction to the dreadful new rich. Wellscombe Manor garaged but two cars, a Daimler and a runabout, and stabled but one hack for Lady Jean and a pony for Elspet. Just to make ends meet the dower-house was let, also one of the lodges. Naturally they were let to friends, but to have to accept rent for them at all was still, or all the more, painful. Sharing every duty as she did with her husband, however, while it was Mr. Lutterel who in-

stalled an old Mrs. Crosby at the dower-house, it was
Lady Jean who installed Jimmy Trevennick at the
lodge.

There is a type of English masculine handsomeness
— elegantly attenuated of limb and skull, dark of hair
and eye, that approximates as nearly to a Velasquez hi-
dalgo as anything to be found in modern Spain. (Not
only bones were washed up, from the Armada.) Such
handsomeness was Jimmy Trevennick's, ex-Guardee, currently stockbroking, but devoted to country pursuits.
Even Cathy, who rather disliked him, had to acknowledge a physical perfection that reputedly caused debs
in their third season to swoon in his arms and chamber-
maids to blush if he spoke to them — as he frequently
did, being always affable to servants. To Cathy he was
particularly affable (which was possibly why she disliked him), asking at once if he might call her Cathy,
but not waiting for permission.

He was some years younger than Lady Jean, which
gave his open admiration of her the character of an acceptable family joke. He was indeed almost part of the
family — strolling up so regularly from his bachelor
quarters at mealtimes, a place was regularly laid for
him. It was he — "Good Jimmy!" murmured Lady Jean
— who was to escort the small domestic party out to
Malta. Obviously Mr. Lutterel couldn't because the
House would be sitting.

4

Such was Lady Jean's immediate apanage, only suitable
to the daughter of a Duke: a husband Member of Parlia-
ment, an exquisite child, a licenced adorer and an attendant sprite. A vicar, a doctor, and old Mrs. Crosby

outerly defended an existence which should have been currently impossible, but in fact was not. If Lady Jean had servant-trouble, she wasn't aware of it. She had a butler. Amongst her defenders Mr. Weaver should indeed have been mentioned earlier. He was a large man, with an eye to subdue and the temperament of a Provost-marshal; from nine in the morning when he served breakfast, to ten o'clock at night when he carried in the ritual Tray of whisky-and-soda and lime-juice, Mr. Weaver's authoritative presence assured all quiet on the domestic front.

In defence of an anachronistic way of life, there is nothing like a good butler.

25

HAPPILY ENTERING THE service of the Madonna, it still didn't take Cathy long to appreciate that a friend who is also a nursery-governess is a nursery-governess first and a friend second; also that the position of the former (as Mrs. Pennon had complained of her own on the Island) is that of neither flesh nor fowl nor good red herring. Cathy breakfasted and lunched above the salt but when it came to dinner was usually accommodated with a tray in the schoolroom. — It wasn't Mr. Weaver who brought it up, but some anonymous housemaid; nor did Cook take much pains. What came up was mostly cold lamb garnished with an offhand sprig of parsley. Cathy munched her way through, however, a volume of Henty propped against the water-jug, happy in the knowledge that at least she wouldn't have to wash up. The freedom from all domestic duties ("Good Cathy, don't lift a *finger!*" implored Lady Jean. "Unless of course you'd like to rinse through Elspet's socks and vests?") was after a year with Muriel a source of happiness in itself; and if any more were needed, wasn't there that little love of an Elspet?

In the big sunny schoolroom —

"Four from seven?" asked Cathy.

"Fwee," lisped Elspet.

Sometimes she lisped and sometimes she didn't. Like her shy fits, her lisp came and went.

"Eight from ten?"

"Two."

"Five from eleven?"

"Have you ever been presented?" asked Elspet.

"No, but I've been to a Governor's fancy-dress ball," said Cathy. "Five from eleven?"

"What as?"

"A Powder-puff," lied Cathy, "in blue satin and swansdown."

"Swansdown's nice," agreed Elspet. "I've been a Snowflake, in swansdown. Was your hair just as red then?"

"As holly-berries," said Cathy. "Five from eleven?"

"What a good idea!" said Elspet admiringly; then paused. "But only if you'd been a Snowflake, like me; not as a Powder-puff . . ."

Obviously she could apply her mind to anything that really interested it. Babyishly bogged down, when it came to spelling, at *c-a-t*, cat, Elspet could whip through a fashion-paper with almost adult expertness; and lisped in back-numbers of the *Tatler*. Her scrap-book with Teddy Bears on the cover contained photographs cut from every recent issue.

"That's me being bridesmaid in Kate Greenaway," pointed out Elspet.

Being bridesmaid was her forte. She figured in wedding-group after wedding-group — and not in groups alone; she had several whole pictures to herself. (Besides being so photogenic she was also delightfully natural. The best and biggest picture showed her gazing in pretty childish dismay at a dropped slice of wedding-cake — caption: *There goes the icing.*) There were also photographs of Elspet on her pony at a gymkhana, of Elspet wearing a big rosette centrally inscribed Vote for Daddy, and a particularly sweet one of Elspet offering her ducal grandfather a birthday sprig of heather . . .

As her Great-aunt Maud once bitingly remarked, she was a regular professional beauty of a child. — It is the mark of the professional to keep in training; even off bridesmaid-duty, even in the sylvan shades of Wellscombe, Elspet lived in a perpetual state of readiness to be photographed. Flitting demure in muslin at tea-time, or scampering from the paddock with a dab of mud on her face like a beauty-spot, Elspet was always on the job. It made it very difficult to teach her anything.

"Good Cathy, didn't I warn you how horrid she was?" sympathized Lady Jean. "She's simply a little exhibitionist — who can't even spell cat!"

The dulcet voice very slightly rebuked. After all, one didn't expect to pay a friend fifteen shillings a week pocket-money and then find one's daughter couldn't spell cat.

"Of course she can," said Cathy, "if she'd try."

"You mean she won't? — That's what Nanny Scott said," recalled Lady Jean worriedly. "She won't concentrate. Can't you *make* her concentrate?"

"Not if she's soon going to be bridesmaid again," said Cathy.

Lady Jean, to her credit, hooted with laughter.

"How well you know her already, my poor babe! What

a treasure you are! Not a single wedding, I promise," said Lady Jean seriously, "before we go to Malta — and till then strict discipline and nursery tea!"

But of course the embargo didn't apply to Conservative bazaars; actually within a week Elspet was peddling lavender-bags in her Kate Greenaway. ("No one's seen it here," explained Elspet. "I've only worn it at St. Margaret's." It was also she, not the photographer, who requested Cathy to stand a little aside.) Cathy's attendance was in fact far more useful to Lady Jean, who always purchased lavishly but never carried anything; Cathy's arms were soon full. — Jimmy Trevennick's arms were filled first, he following more closely at her ladyship's heels; to Cathy fell the overflow, usually bulkier and stickier: tea-cosies, pots of jam, honey in the comb. By a peculiar misfortune Lady Jean guessed correctly the weight of a fruit-cake and won a sucking-pig. The innocent baby-faced creature had at least had its throat cut, but Jimmy Trevennick, ex-Guards, unloaded it on Cathy with speed. "Good Cathy, can you *bear* it?" cried Lady Jean — not only literally. "It's from one of the farms we had to sell — so *not* to be refused? Good Cathy," begged Lady Jean, "for heaven's sake put it under the tea-cosies!"

Cathy swallowed and did her best, but still the trotters dangled. It was actually Miss Palmer from the Post Office, with no business there at all, who found a hamper. "You're new, Miss Pennon," said Miss Palmer kindly, "or you'd know always to bring one with you. *Last* year her ladyship won a live goose."

The single real contact Cathy made with Lady Jean's husband occurred late one night upon his return from London. Cathy was in fact about to go to bed. She had, unusually, dined downstairs, with Lady Jean and Jimmy
Trevennick — absolutely pressed to do so, by Lady Jean
— but when after the Tray a rug was turned back in the
drawing-room and the gramophone put on, she felt superfluous. "Why not teach *Cathy* the tango?" suggested
Lady Jean kindly. "Like a shot!" agreed Mr. Trevennick.
Cathy still felt superfluous, and mumbling something
about Elspet's perhaps being awake (which Lady Jean
did not seriously contest), took herself upstairs. The
child as it happened was sleeping like a dormouse; Cathy
removed a *Tatler* from the pillow, went on to her own
room, and only then remembered a pair of gloves left
not in, but upon, the Bible-box. So she went downstairs
again.

In the hall, the heart of the house, the fire had for
once gone out. It was always a little cold, even in summer, in the marble-flagged hall; without a fire, Cathy
shivered. From behind the drawing-room door music still
sounded — not the tango now, but an old-fashioned Viennese waltz. Cathy stood a moment beside the Bible-
box, gloves in hand, listening to the amorous pulsating
rhythm; then raised the heavy oak lid carved with Adam
and Eve, dropped her gloves inside and reascended
the stair. As always, on the landing she paused; and so
saw Mr. Lutterel come home.

Weaver the butler, who had doubtless heard the car,
was there to open up. — Cathy had a fancy that Mr.
Lutterel liked to employ his own big iron key himself;

but there Weaver was. She distinguished a brief exchange: Mr. Lutterel, it appeared, had dined on the train. Weaver before withdrawing performed some rather fancy locking-up, which his employer, to Cathy's eye, regarded with some impatience. — She made no move herself, however; she expected Mr. Lutterel to go straight into the drawing-room, and meanwhile the sight of him standing temporarily isolated in the heart of his house was curiously impressive . . .

Just as Cathy had done, Mr. Lutterel stood listening. The tune audible from the drawing-room was still a waltz. Mr. Lutterel listened for some moments; then walked across to the cold hearth and kicked apart the ash-whitened logs. Then he mounted the broad stair and found Cathy on the landing.

She had turned away as he came up; their looks met in the mirror between the tapestries. Though its surface was dimmed by time it still reflected accurately enough, as they stood side by side, the one's long nose, the other's rough red head.

"We're neither of us beauties," said Mr. Lutterel. "Good night to you."

26

I N THE BIG sunny schoolroom —
    "Pony?" asked Cathy.
    "P-o-n-y," spelled Elspet.
    "Gymkhana?"
    The child absolutely rattled it off.
    "And cat?"
    "K-a-t."
Cathy sometimes gave a curious thought to her predecessor Nanny Scott; there was so little about Elspet to suggest any period of training at the hands of a tremendously qualified nursery-nurse. The child indeed appeared to have no more recollection of her departed instructress than of a departed Siamese — rather less: the photograph of Elspet hiding her face in Ho's fur at the Cat Show, caption A pair of shy kittens, was firmly pasted into her scrap-book. Nor could Cathy, now that she knew Lady Jean better, visualize her employer being terrorized by any nurse whatever short of Florence Nightingale. What had happened, in short, to Nanny Scott? It is a question all governesses naturally put, in reference to their predecessors; and though at first Cathy flinched from pumping the child, curiosity at last overcame delicacy.

"Was Nanny Scott very strict with you?" suggested Cathy.

Elspet looked up from the current issue of *Vogue*. (She didn't enjoy it so much as the *Tatler*, there were fewer people she knew in it, but the current issue of the *Tatler* still reposed in Lady Jean's parlour. Elspet knew she wouldn't have to wait long for it, however. Family affection is sometimes presumed to glow warmer in slum than stately home, and indeed often does, but just as mother and daughter in a slum swap comics, so Lady Jean and Elspet swapped glossies.)

"No; but she had freckles," said Elspet. — "Not like yours," she added hastily, discarding *Vogue* to run and look up in Cathy's face just as though there were a photographer about. "Not just a few nice little freckles like you have, huge big brown ones all over her hands, because she was about a hundred years old . . ."

With more precision, Cathy visualized an attendant sprite still light of foot (light as an autumn leaf), but crumpling under the weight of a sucking-pig. Evidently what had happened to Nanny Scott was simply that she'd grown too old to be any use.

The only physical traces Cathy discovered of her predecessor confirmed this impression: a few bent grey hairpins left under the paper of a bureau drawer. On her palm they weighed nothing; it was absurd that they should weigh on her mind. Cathy had no fears of herself growing old and grey in the Madonna's service, she was going to skip ship; her dismay was that of the worshipper suddenly perceiving a flaw in the worshipped image. Cold mutton on a tray hadn't damaged it, nor solitary evenings spent reading Henty; but this was a moment when Cathy recalled that for her first quarter's salary, at

142

fifteen shillings a week, she'd just received a cheque for nine pounds.

Pulling out the drawer to its extreme limit, however, she released a small diary jammed behind. It wasn't sensational. There was no reason why Nanny Scott, discovering it left behind, should have lost sleep. It contained in fact very few entries at all, and those for the most part obviously reminders of family birthdays, prudently noted a day or two in advance. (*"Cousin Sarah's birthday, next Wed.; Uncle Henry's, next Fri."*) Only once did the small neat handwriting run across a couple of days — the fourth and fifth of May, or almost exactly a month before Cathy's own arrival. *"Uncle Henry passed on to his Maker. May his soul rest in peace and I be kept humble in prosperity. Mem: Solicitors Graham and Graham, 14, Ellenborough Place, flowers to McGillivray's, 42, Castle Street, funeral Sat. . . .*

The load on Cathy's heart and mind lifted as she realized that Nanny Scott hadn't been dismissed after all but had obviously retired of her own accord to enjoy an antimacassared retirement. — Forgivingly the image of the Madonna smiled again, scarcely chiding a worshipper's brief lapse of faith.

2

Of course there were occasions when to chide was necessary. One difficulty about doubling the rôles of governess and attendant sprite is that whereas the latter is expected to be omnipresent, of the former the very reverse is required: it was small wonder that Cathy, socially awkward in any case, now and then made a gaffe — missing, for example, when the League of International Friendship sent a foreign visitor to tea, but all too present at one Sunday lunch when the Vicar came. The hymn had been the one about Ceylon's Happy Isle; Cathy absolutely interrupted the Vicar, who was chatting about the Liberal vote, to observe that its total area including outlying islands was more than three-quarters that of Ireland and it had five million inhabitants. "Indeed?" said the Vicar courteously. "Mostly Buddhist," said Cathy. "Elspet's certainly going to know all about Ceylon!" cried Lady Jean. "Let Weaver give you a little more soufflé, Vicar . . ."

She still chid Cathy very tactfully, not bidding her in so many words to hold her tongue at table, but simply pointing out that if there was one thing a parson didn't want at Sunday lunch it was religion. Lady Jean never forgot that besides being a nursery-governess and an attendant sprite, Cathy was also a friend.

3

Muriel never forgot it either. What her sister's exact salary was she never discovered, Cathy's letter asking for her box to be sent didn't mention it; but the information that she was to be received on the footing of a friend, if it caused Archy to raise his eye-brows, was to Muriel a source of much innocent snobbish pleasure. — "Where's Cathy?" asked Judith Bamber. "Staying with Lady Jean," said Muriel. "*Staying?*" repeated Judith suspiciously. "I thought she'd applied to go as governess?" "That was just Miss McCorquodale's idea," smiled Muriel, "but obviously *too* ridiculous!" "Especially when she didn't even pass Matric.," agreed Judith. "Archy and I still thought it would do her good to try her wings a little," explained Muriel — rather jumping a gap. "Lady Jean took such a liking to her, now she's there just as a friend . . ."

Judith Bamber was the hardest nut to crack, but as the weeks and months passed, and no Cathy returned sacked and hang-dog, even Judith accepted the pleasing myth. With less intimate acquaintances Muriel had no trouble at all. — "My sister? Don't ask me when we'll ever see her again!" sighed Muriel. "She's gone off to her friend Lady Jean . . ."

Even the infant Anna was taught the shibboleth. "Who loves her Aunt Cathy?" reminded, or persuaded Muriel. "Little Anna! — And where's Aunt Cathy now?"

Evidently little Anna couldn't be expected to reply, Wellscombe Manor, Wellscombe Halt, Devon, so Muriel curtailed the answer for her.

"With Lady Jean!" cried Muriel.

She often thought of running down to pay Cathy a little visit; but despite every hint no invitation came, and Archy rather frowned on the notion of taking the Lutterels by surprise. Also the summer had ended, and almost the autumn. It was November.

27

CATHY HAD CHILBLAINS. It was inexplicable: November in Devon wasn't particularly cold, only wet. — Were there any late autumnal scenes by Birket Foster, wondered Cathy? Kate Greenaway children in muffs and tippets she recalled distinctly, but always against a background of snow and red-berried holly; in Devon, in November, it was rather Tosti who hit the mark with his falling leaf and fading tree. The woods behind the Manor began to drip, the buttercup-fields to dissolve in plash. It still wasn't nearly cold enough to warrant chilblains. Shamefacedly Cathy bandaged her knuckles and stomached equally Elspet's wrinkled nose, the despising glances of Mr. Weaver, and the jokes of Jimmy Trevennick, who pretended to see her as a flyweight boxer. Lady Jean, who very much hoped her attendant sprite wasn't going to turn out sickly, more kindly suggested a tonic, and Dr. James made one up which Cathy took punctually three times a day. — "You've a poor circulation, young woman," said Dr. James. "So would you have," retorted Cathy obscurely, and with a touch of her old ferocity. However at the end of the next few weeks (during which there coincidentally arrived for Lady Jean several leaflets from the P. and O. Line), her chilblains healed.

2

"Where's Cathy? Where's my good Cathy?" warbled Lady Jean.

Even in November there was sun in Lady Jean's parlour. It had been specially built for her, to jut east, south and west. Sunlight however watery haloed her golden head; on the desk by her side lay a deck-cabin plan. As Cathy paused on the threshold she felt the same slight sickness that had overtaken her at St. Anne's Mansions; only now there was no possibility, so to speak, that the Governor wouldn't be at home . . .

"Sit down, dear," said Lady Jean, "and let's have a little discussion."

"I don't mind going second," said Cathy quickly.

"My dear, I'm sure you wouldn't!" cried Lady Jean. "That's what's so sweet about you — you always *understand!* But I've been thinking; and *what* I've been thinking is, why should you and poor little Elspet be dragged to Malta at all?"

3

Cathy sat. Beside her, at her elbow, the desk was strewn with plans of boat-decks, promenade-decks, swimming-pools; the whole anatomy of a vessel designed for carrying passengers towards the sun. The only plan lacking was that of the engine-room, without which the vessel couldn't sail at all.

"Probably the climate wouldn't suit either of you," continued Lady Jean. "I've just been selfish, wanting

147

you with me. But now, as I say, I've *thought*; and I've decided not to be selfish any more."

Cathy swallowed.

"It's a perfectly healthy climate. I was brought up — isn't it partly why you hired me? — on the Next-door Island myself."

"But to the ruin of your circulation," pointed out Lady Jean. "I mean, chilblains in November! I couldn't possibly risk Elspet getting chilblains."

"She wouldn't get chilblains any more than she'd get Malta fever," argued Cathy stubbornly.

"Well, perhaps not," admitted Lady Jean. "But there's the *uprooting* too. I've been reading all about it. I read much more and much more seriously," said Lady Jean, thrusting the current issue of *Vogue* a little behind her, "than anyone realizes. What a child needs above all is a stable, rooted background and not to be skated off to Malta at a mother's whim. You shall be left in complete charge, my dear, and if that doesn't show my confidence in you I don't know what does."

Still Cathy couldn't quite believe it.

"And not go to Malta?"

"My good Cathy, haven't I just been explaining it all to you?" protested Lady Jean, with a touch of impatience. "You can't really be so stupid! *I* go to Malta, you and Elspet stay here."

"What about Mr. Trevennick?" asked Cathy.

"Naturally good Jimmy comes, to escort me. I can't travel alone. — Once I'm there of course I shall be staying at the Palace," added Lady Jean lightly, "perfectly *surrounded* by aide-de-camps! — so he'll be able to spend every *minute* playing polo . . ."

Wooden as an image sat Cathy in her chair: rocked

148

not physically, like the image of the Madonna on the men's shoulders, but mentally, by the knowledge she'd been made a fool of. Her employer, Cathy suddenly, bleakly, realized, had never intended to take her to Malta; Malta had been simply one more bait to hook an underpaid attendant sprite. Lady Jean had always intended to go to Malta alone — with Jimmy Trevennick.

Of course to stay at the Palace. No scandal: only the eight days' trip each way; first approaching ever nearer to the sun, then the gentle elegaic withdrawal as the gold on their skins faded and they practised — with what moments of sweet backsliding? — the colder manners of the north. What a hobble she and Elspet would have been, thought Cathy, a child and a governess — the one all too observant, the other all too simple!

Lady Jean also had fallen into a muse. Melting already under the sun — her lids drooped, her lips a little parted — she looked less like the Madonna than like Danäe expectant. With an impulse of pure iconoclasm —

"I'm leaving," said Cathy. "Now. I don't have to give notice, because I'm here just as a friend."

Incredulously the sea-blue eyes opened.

"But you can't!" cried Lady Jean. "Don't you know Elspet simply *dotes* on you? Besides," she added, more realistically, "without a reference what would you *do*?"

"What I was doing before," said Cathy. "Corky didn't exactly find me begging in the streets."

"Now you're getting cross," chided Lady Jean, "and I shan't listen to a single word more, it wouldn't be *fair*, till you're your nice, good self again . . ."

To ensure which she rose and floated from the room, leaving Cathy in possession.

Of course Cathy hadn't been begging in the streets. She'd been living in an exceptionally comfortable home with her own room and her own gas-fire and her own subscription to Boots'. Besides the pleasure of living in a house so polished that a polishing-rag wore out inside a month there'd been the pleasure of having such a little love of a niece; brooding over all a sister's protective kindness as evinced in suggestions of taking dressmaking classes and going to Harrods. When Cathy remembered all the comforts to which (considering Muriel's conscientiousness) she had no doubt she might return, her heart sank.

She'd got away once, through the intervention of Corky. She could hardly expect Corky to intervene again, Lady Jean withholding a reference. Back to the Maclarens might well mean back to the Maclarens for life. Cathy genuinely felt she sooner would indeed beg in the streets.

But how did one begin, to beg in the streets? It is a phrase used commonly enough, under the stress of emotion, but rarely examined with any realism. Cathy, unusually, did so. She remembered beggars enough on the Next-door Island — bundles of rag and bone stretching forth maimed, emaciated claws; but they seemed to have been born to the profession. So did the rarer hymn-singer in the streets of a London suburb. Immediately to set forth on the Plymouth road with outstretched hand would almost certainly provoke the offer of a lift from Dr. James or the Vicar. (Or even chauffeur-driven Mrs. Crosby.) "A lift, Miss Pennon?" Cathy heard each cry — but couldn't hear herself answer, "No, thank you,

I'm begging." She might indeed achieve London — she had sufficient funds for the railway-fare — and start begging there; even so, the sheer mechanics of the thing daunted her. Did one for instance need a licence to beg, as to peddle? Would the placard DISTRESSED EX-GOVERNESS be acceptable in Oxford Street? — A long-ago memory stirring, Cathy as on the day of Mr. Pennon's funeral glanced towards the simpler status of tramp. (The answer, "No, thank you, I'm tramping," at least momentarily comprehensible to Dr. James, Mrs. Crosby and the Vicar.) Even as she examined these projects Cathy recognized them for the fantasies they were; and that unless one was bred to begging or the road, deliberately to become a beggar or a tramp was as difficult as to become a chartered accountant. She simply hadn't been indentured . . .

At this moment in her meditations the door opened on Mr. Weaver. He carried the big silver tea-tray with all its usual appurtenances, but only, Cathy noted, one cup: which left room for a silver muffineer and a pot of Gentleman's Relish.

"Her ladyship expects you to take tea in here, miss," said Weaver.

Cathy recognized the sort of bare-faced bribery employed in pocket-boroughs. No doubt Lady Jean's ducal family — possibly Mr. Lutterel's also — had an inherited technique for dealing with pocket-boroughs, crude but effective. Whence Cathy had inherited the instincts of an honest freeholder (or Luddite) was more problematic; in any case, before she could dash the tray from Mr. Weaver's hands he had set it down and withdrawn.

More coolly, Cathy recognized that had she done so it

would have been less from principle than from temper. (However clever the Lutterels at handling pocket-boroughs, Strathspeys were undoubtedly cleverer.) She was tired from emotion, and the hot tea invited, if only to clear her mind . . .

So did the muffins invite. Like Persephone biting into a pomegranate, and so consigning herself to the realms of Dis, Cathy bit into a muffin.

It marked the nadir of her morale since she'd left the Next-door Island. — Lady Jean was wonderfully under-standing. She didn't even expect an apology. "Good Cathy, I didn't realize how disappointed you'd be!" cried Lady Jean. "I feel it is *I* who should apologize to *you!*"

A week later she was gone. Mr. Lutterel happened to be on duty at Westminster, so wasn't there to see Jimmy drive her off in his sports car from the Manor door. (Lady Jean's instinct for marrying effrontery with discretion amounted to genius.) Nor was Elspet there either, having had a flaming row with her mummy over being left behind. In the great porch flanked by drip-ping laurels only a governess and butler stood to atten-tion — and Lady Jean, like a French general present-ing medals, kissed Cathy on both cheeks.

"All, all in your charge, good Cathy!" cried Lady Jean. "What a treasure you are!"

After the car had driven off Cathy observed in the drive an old shoe. She could only imagine that some tramp had lost his way, and turned back, and passed on.

152

28

IT MAY BE SAID at once that Mr. Lutterel did not fall in love with Cathy nor she with him. The one was no more a Rochester than the other a Jane Eyre. Indeed, on the few occasions when they lunched alone together her employer courteously asked permission to bring a *Hansard* to table; Cathy brought a Henty; and with *Hansard* at one end and Henty at the other the meal commonly passed in complete silence. This period however marked a definite change in Cathy's life at Wellscombe — though whether for better or worse is debatable.

Lady Jean, in her solicitude for her husband's comfort, whenever he was at home, and hadn't work to do after dinner, was always ready for a game of bridge. So was Jimmy Trevennick always ready, and if no one was staying she summoned the doctor or the Vicar or at a pinch old Mrs. Crosby. One evening immediately after her return from Malta, however, none of these faithfuls was available; Dr. James was attending a confinement, the Vicar was attending a death-bed, and Mrs. Crosby had a cold. Lady Jean, while mentally lumping all these excuses together under the heading of Tiresomeness, was still forced to accept them; and with the bridge-table set out and her husband already seated, bethought her of her attendant sprite.

"Cathy it must be," decided Lady Jean. "If she doesn't play, she must learn: we might need her again. — I suppose one can't exactly *ring* for her!" added Lady Jean wryly. "And I hate disturbing Weaver before the Tray. — I'll run up myself."

With her customary sweet fluency of movement she was out of the room as Jimmy made to open the door. He returned and sat down in his usual place: facing Mr. Lutterel across the square of green baize. Neither had found anything to say to the other, before Lady Jean floated back looking slightly ruffled.

"It's the most extraordinary thing," exclaimed Lady Jean, "but she isn't *there*. She isn't *in* the schoolroom. And she isn't in her bedroom either, because I've looked."

"She has crept out," suggested Jimmy Trevennick, "to keep a secret rendezvous with the curate of the next parish."

"Don't be silly, darling," said Lady Jean, rather sharply. "That would be Mr. Martin."

"Whom we all know chained to your chariot-wheels already," agreed Jimmy. "How far your little candle shines! — Or am I mixing my metaphors?" he added, to Mr. Lutterel. "I mean, *can* a moth be chained to chariot-wheels?"

"Not to much purpose, perhaps," said Mr. Lutterel.

"Then we must just play three-handed," said Lady Jean, sitting down and rapidly dealing the cards.

2

So was Mr. Weaver dealing, below stairs: but only five cards apiece, for poker; then he held the rest of the pack suspended while Cook chose her discard.

"One, if you please, Mr. Weaver."

"Drawing to a broken straight again?" rebuked Henry the chauffeur. "I'll take three . . ."

"Drawing to a full house?" enquired Mr. Weaver blandly.

May the upper housemaid took two, Janice her colleague four.

"I'll stand," said Cathy.

Once again, as on Victoria Avenue, she had thrown in her lot with the Natives.

3

Rare as is the governess who plays poker at all, still rarer is one who plays it with the servants. Yet it came about very naturally. Cathy, one evening shortly after Lady Jean's departure, had as usual dined in the school-room; some hour later, pathetic cries from the night-nursery summoned her to find that Elspet had decided she was getting Malta fever. (There was an ingenuity about this almost worthy of admiration, and undoubtedly the child had managed to make herself very hot; she lay tossing against the frilled pillows scarlet in the face.) "I've got Malta fever," whimpered Elspet, "send a wire to Mummy." "Rubbish," said Cathy. (*"You little brute, you little beast, you little pest,"* she added mentally. — Not aloud; Elspet, unlike little Anna, was the grand-daughter of a Duke. Cathy had become more corrupted than she knew; which made her subsequent behaviour all the more surprising.) "And to Daddy at the House, and get Dr. James," added Elspet, widening her field. "Rubbish," repeated Cathy — at least not so sufficiently corrupted as to bedevil two over-worked men on behalf of a child's injured ego. "I'll fetch you a glass of milk and you can have half an aspirin it in . . ."

So she took a short cut down the back stairs. One of the disadvantages of so old a house as Wellscombe was the lack of a proper servants' hall. Mr. Weaver had his butler's pantry, but for all social life condescended to the kitchen. It was fortunately on his own scale; so enormous, a cantle about the size of a modern luxury-flat could be devoted to the poker, ex-dining, table. About this, as Cathy entered, butler and cook, chauffeur and two housemaids all courteously rose — incidentally screening five glasses and a bottle of Mr. Lutterel's best port. Cathy's eye with equal courtesy omitted the port, but lighted on a straight flush just laid down by Cook.

"What did you draw to?" asked Cathy inquisitively.

"Lacking the seven," confessed Cook.

"I shouldn't have had the nerve," said Cathy.

"You mean, the foolhardiness," said Mr. Weaver. "Do you happen to play yourself, miss?"

"I used to," said Cathy.

Mr. Weaver paused. He glanced round the table, silently taking the opinion of the company. They had often agreed that six made a better game, but also that it was out of the question to admit Bridie the between-maid to the pleasures of her superiors; moreover when her ladyship needed Henry to drive at night there was no poker at all. — Cook, who had been performing the same office as her colleague, slightly nodded.

"Should you ever care to join us, miss," said Mr. Weaver graciously, "you'll generally find a game going between dinner and the Tray. In fact, during her lady-ship's absence, we can get down to it sooner."

"What time?" asked Cathy eagerly.

"While the House sits, eight P.M. sharp."

So down Cathy slipped each night by the back stairs for a couple of refreshing hours; and thanks to Jacko was universally respected for her strict, classic game. — If Elspet wanted to have Malta fever, let her, thought Cathy, dosing her charge with a whole aspirin. Elspet slept like a top, Cathy played poker; and even after Lady Jean's return, as has been seen, continued an esteemed member of Mr. Weaver's school.

4

There was still, naturally, an inquest over the breakfast-table next morning. Another of Lady Jean's virtues was that she never breakfasted in bed. Punctually at nine o'clock there she sat, in tweeds and cashmere, complete to single row of pearls, ready to pour coffee for herself and her husband and tea for Cathy and Elspet . . .

"What a lovely crisp day!" exclaimed Lady Jean, "and how sweet and fresh you look, good Cathy, just matching it! By the way, where *were* you," she added, "last night after dinner? I looked in the schoolroom, I looked in your bedroom —"

Mr. Lutterel was reading *The Times*, Elspet drawing her initials in cream on a plate of porridge. Weaver, at the side-table, slightly turned.

"I expect in the kitchen," said Cathy cheerfully.

"In the *kitchen?*" repeated Lady Jean incredulously.

"Below-stairs."

"But—"

"Fetching Elspet a glass of milk."

The child's spoon paused in the middle of a curlicue.

"I didn't have any milk, last night . . ."

"You'd gone to sleep again," reminded Cathy. — "I'm afraid it's a bad habit we got into while you were away," she apologized, to her employer. "Elspet did so miss Mummy at bye-byes!"

If Elspet had been about to argue, the picture was far too pretty to pass up.

"I cried all through my prayers," she accused. "Cathy had to give me half an aspirin."

"Only once," said Cathy, quite truthfully.

"*And* I was getting Malta fever," remembered Elspet.

"Don't be silly," said Lady Jean impatiently — also with an eye on the leader-page of *The Times*, which Mr. Lutterel had so folded as to read the main news first. "I've never seen you looking healthier — and I'm sure I'm just as grateful to Cathy as you should be!"

She still, breakfast over, drifted upstairs to the night-nursery. But Mr. Weaver had been before her: on the table by the frilled pillow stood an untouched glass of milk.

29

THEY WERE AN odd lot, a job lot, below-stairs. Only Cook had any tradition of good service. Henry the chauffeur-cum-groom had served in India. Both May and Janice were ex-munitions; Cook often remarked that if they'd made shells as they made beds we'd never have won the war. As for Bridie from Ireland, in Mr. Weaver's opinion she'd never been under a roof. Only he, great man that he was, could have bullied and jockeyed them all into some decent semblance of a staff — deferring to Cook, slamming down Henry, encouraging Bridie, sleeping alternately with Janice and May. Cathy never became entirely integrated amongst them — her different duties, above-stairs, made it impossible; but she was soon quite a leading light.

As has been said, her strict, classic poker won universal respect; what made her popular was her ability to mimic her employer. — Cathy hadn't intended to embark on such a course, the first time she fluted out "Pass!" on Lady Jean's exact warbling note, but the resultant laughter went to her head. "O for just one little attendant knave!" warbled Cathy, laying down two jacks and a pair of tens. "Tut-tut! — Barley-water, Jean?" suggested Weaver — impersonating Mr. Lutterel. "Or gin-

and-tonic, my sweet?" suggested Henry — impersonating Jimmy Trevennick; and Cathy found herself playing not only poker but also that age-old below-stairs game, so old that it dates from the Saturnalia, of servant mimicking master . . .

The play was far more exciting below-stairs than at the bridge-table above. Often a pound or two changed hands before the bell summoned Mr. Weaver with the Tray; who putting away score-blocks frequently memorized such petty sums as three-and-ninepence (Lutterel and the Rev. down). Cathy added at least ten bob a week to her salary.

2

Everything was more exciting, below-stairs. Just as on the Island, above-stairs a small garrison held the fort of gentility while below pullulated the rich, natural life of the Natives. All emotion, for example, was shown more nakedly: Bridie at a fancied insult from May went into hysterics, between May and Janice, superficially bosom-friends, a vendetta concerning Mr. Weaver's favours constantly smouldered and about once a month exploded. Mr. Weaver philosophically retired to his pantry while the plates flew, but when Henry chanced his arm and drove May for an outing in the Daimler no further than Taunton, the Daimler's tyres were subsequently, mysteriously, let down. (Like Jacko, Mr. Weaver had a touch of the Mafia about him.) Even Cook could be uninhibited of language if the fish didn't come. Especially if Janice and May were still at daggers drawn, and Henry looking at Mr. Weaver as though he'd like to murder him, if the fish was late Cook didn't like Vatel commit suicide, but her language, (as all in cooler moments admiringly agreed), was proper Billingsgate.

"I sometimes marvel where you learnt it," once observed Mr. Weaver over the poker-table, "you as you often remark having spent your life in good service?"

"Maybe in early youth given a poll-parrot by a Bristol sailor," suggested Henry.

"I only wish us'd been given poll-parrots, 'stead of they frippery mats," said Janice.

"Maltese lace is famous," rebuked Cook. "(One, if you please, Mr. Weaver.) In my opinion her ladyship was very good to remember the staff at all, on her little excursion."

"Or honeymoon," said Henry. "I'll take four."

"Mad," said Mr. Weaver, "but on your own head be it. May?"

"Four to me too," giggled May. "I must say they drove off in style!"

"Miss Pennon, by the look of her, will stand," said Mr. Weaver. "Am I right or wrong?"

Cathy however didn't immediately answer. She had suddenly remembered something. There was a slight pause, while Weaver held the pack suspended.

"That shoe in the drive . . . Was it you who threw it?"

"Not I," said Mr. Weaver virtuously. "Perish, I may add, the thought. It was that perishing Henry."

"And didn't he do it neat?" giggled May. "Janice and me saw it all, Miss Pennon, from upstairs. He was just by you against the porch."

"Camouflaged as a laurel," agreed Henry.

"Showing off before the girls," rebuked Cook.

"Who said it ought to be a horse-shoe in white heather?" retorted Henry.

"Cook did!" giggled May.

"Only as a passing joke," said Cook, "as Mr. Weaver will bear out."

"May and me thought of rice," recalled Janice.

"Wilful waste breeds woeful want," said Cook severely.

"Anyway, us never *meant* Henry — did us, Janice?" protested May.

"Trust the women to egg a chap on and then throw him over," said Henry cynically. "I should ha' learnt my lesson among the mems. '*Poor boy!*' " he fluted, in a sudden feminine tremolo. " '*How simply ghastly — where's my ayah? — to have to ask you to hook me up behind!*' Then squeals and a rap over the knuckles."

"Pipe down," said Mr. Weaver. "Her ladyship having returned amongst us with unblemished reputation —"

"Says who?" jeered Henry.

"*I* do," said Mr. Weaver, fixing him with a Provost Marshal's eye. "Now where's that perishing Tray?"

It was extraordinary how different, from below-stairs, appeared the image of the Madonna. Equally different from an accepted image would above-stairs have found below; its loyalty no more suspect than that of an Indian regiment before the Mutiny.

3

Occasionally, after some particularly successful impersonation of her employer, Cathy felt slightly ashamed. But never for long. Her new character as a subversive element carried too many advantages. — There was for example the immediate improvement in her suppers:

instead of cold mutton, Cook sent up toothsome little fricassees, now and then a wing of chicken, at the very least an omelette stuffed with mushrooms; in due course, as the shooting season opened and game began to arrive from Strathspey, cold grouse. But of all her new privileges, the one Cathy most appreciated was hearing Mr. Weaver on the telephone.

Like all butlers, he spoke two distinct tongues — his native and his official. Naturally above-stairs never heard the first, nor below-stairs the second; Cathy, if she happened to be passing through the hall as he lifted the receiver, was privileged to hear him make the actual switch. — "Lady Duff?" intoned Weaver dulcetly. "To speak to her ladyship? — Ex-Navy and thinks she's Nelson," added Weaver, cupping his hand over the mouthpiece. "Cheats at bridge, dear, also marge in the servants' hall. — Certainly, m'lady; I shall just need to seek her ladyship in the rose-garden. — Where you won't find *me* skating about, not in this heat," added Weaver, laying the receiver down and taking a little time off to polish his nails. Sometimes he took enough time off to empty a few ashtrays; or enough time off to give a more extended character-sketch — as, for example, of the Honourable Mrs. Tablet. "Artistic nude," glossed Weaver. "Nobbled the Hon. when too pie-eyed to tell a registrar's from a fire-station. But very respectable all the same, like most nudes, and now hubby's on the waggon . . ."

"How d'you know she was a nude?" asked Cathy, fascinated.

" 'Saw her myself, dear, wearing nothing but the Eiffel Tower on her head. She was the Spirit of Gay Paree . . ."

No less fascinated was Cathy by Mr. Weaver's histrionic pants (as of one who has just searched a rose-garden) as he begged Lady Duff's pardon, reported her ladyship not to be found, and asked for a message. — "Which is the same as usual," reported Weaver, "gout signals raised and can't dine. Nelson or not, the poor bag has her trials."

"But I bet she still hunts," coughed Cathy.

She never encountered the Duffs, however, nor any other of the Manor's dinner-guests; as Lady Jean reflected, no one ever minded an extra *man*; and good Cathy really *was* rather tactless; and besides didn't own an evening dress, and Lady Jean was far too sensible to expect her to buy one on thirty pounds a year. Cathy's only social experience derived from Sunday teas when the League of International Friendship sent a foreign visitor — many of whom must have left under the impression that Lady Jean in her benevolence sheltered a deaf-mute. A dinner-party at the Manor, to Cathy, meant simply no poker.

All below-stairs took the same view. As Mr. Weaver magisterially pronounced, it was a poor neighbourhood. — Janice reported Mrs. Tablet in her black for the third time running, the Hon. still on the waggon was practically an insult to decent claret. Admiral Duff, gout permitting, cracked a naval joke or two, but scoffed down a bisque d'homard like so much loblolly; other, lesser constituents in Cook's opinion couldn't tell a salmi from a shepherd's pie. It was therefore only natural that the arrival of His Grace of Strathspey to dine and sleep should cause a certain stir.

Actually the stir was considerable. As Lady Jean agitatedly explained, the Duke was so simple. He was so simple, the big guest-room newly-redecorated in cream and apricot would utterly dismay him: so down came the cream velvet curtains, up went a set of almost threadbare tapestry, out went quilted satin bedhead and matching coverlet, in came brass and candlewick. Dinner too was to be as simple as possible — absolutely no guests, not even Jimmy Trevennick, just a family party of the Lutterels and the Duke; and since he would arrive only in time to dress, Cathy was to bring Elspet in with the coffee.

"Of course she should be asleep," pleaded Lady Jean, "but it *is* her grandfather! Good Cathy, if you'd just pop her down in her little nightie — ?"

Cathy was only too glad of the chance to get a look at the Duke herself; she felt a considerable curiosity about him both as Lady Jean's parent and Corky's second-cousin. As for Elspet, she was good as gold — also as intelligent as her mother: already in a frilly nightgown, she of her own accord burrowed into a bottom drawer to produce, and change into, one of plain white flannel, slightly shrunk. It was really a pity there was no photographer about, as innocent in white flannel, cherubically beautiful, the child conquered a moment's shyness and ran into her grandfather's lap . . .

Or rather, such was her intention; only the Duke happened to be on his feet. — Tall, thin, a face all bone and breeding, Cathy fleetingly saw him as a gaunt old stag much bayed about but still monarch of his glen; was equally fleetingly surprised to catch the same sort of look about Mr. Lutterel at his father-in-law's side. Since both were standing, Elspet couldn't even run into daddy's lap and peep at Grandpa over Daddy's shoulder; but she did the next best thing by hugging Grandpa's knees.

"Here's Elspet!" cried Lady Jean. "Come for just a good-night kiss!"

The Duke stooped. Elspet strained up on pretty tiptoes and hugged him now round the neck. Any glossy in London would have given them a spread.

"My poor poppet!" murmured Lady Jean. "My puir penniless lass —" (like her butler she had two voices, one southern county English, one Scots) — "wi' a lang pedigree! I often ask myself what's going to become of her."

"Mightn't she learn to type?" suggested His Grace. "I hear that in Edinburgh typists earn three pounds a week."

He was evidently inoculated against the family charm. (Like his son-in-law, he'd married the most beautiful woman of her generation.) He was a wise old bird — or stag. Cathy, recognizing in him something of the Governor's tolerant, disabused wisdom, felt she would have enjoyed a long talk with him. But His Grace, having once acknowledged her presence by a courteous nod, recalled it only with the suggestion that Elspet should be taken back to bed. — The latter, equally frustrated, had at least the resource of tripping in her nightgown and so being momentarily at least upheld in ducal arms; Cathy could but do as she was bid.

"Poor Gwandpa!" lisped Elspet, out of flannel and into frills again. "Mummy says he's tewwibly pwessed for money."

"Nonsense, he must be worth a million," said Cathy bracingly.

"But all in land," pointed out Elspet. (It occurred to Cathy to wonder whether besides reading *Vogue* and the *Tatler* her charge ever dipped into the *Financial Times*. The phrase had more probably been overheard, however, in some conversation between Elspet's parents; like the one that followed.) "You don't *own* entailed land, the land owns you," explained Elspet. "Poor Grandpa! I can't go to sleep for worrying about him; you must read me out of *Peter Pan*."

She snuggled back against the pillow, her beautiful aquamarine eyes — her mother's eyes — resolutely open, her exquisite, still-babyish mouth resolutely shut to show that however sorry for poor Grandpa she meant to be brave and not cry. But Cathy no less than His Grace was inoculated against the family charm.

"Either go to sleep, or darn well lie awake," said Cathy, snapping off the light.

30

UNDOUBTEDLY ELSPET'S GOVERNESS had
grown less conscientious. In the big sunny schoolroom —

"You can read perfectly well," said Cathy. "Here's
Lamb's *Tales from Shakespeare* and when I come back
you can tell me the plots."

With that she took herself off for a spell of sun-
bathing on the roof.

2

It was an ideal spot she had discovered, some nine
square feet of leads (or about the size of the Governor's
balcony) between the parapet of the house and a shel-
tering stack of chimneys. By afternoon on any sunny day
the leads would be almost hot; sometimes Cathy brought
out a quilt, sometimes she didn't, but took the heat as
directly on her naked back as the sun on her face. The
old brick of the twisted chimneys also stored, and
breathed out, heat; Cathy stripped in a temperature
about that of a conservatory, or Harrods. — This being
before the bikini era, she simply stripped.

Hotly beat the sun on her small, still skinny frame;
baked her brains. That Elspet was probably reading not

Lamb but V*ogue* disturbed not a whit Elspet's governess stark naked on the Manor roof. The only thing Cathy
kept on was a wrist-watch, to check how much time she
had left before tea; but in fact the shadow of the chimneys told her, like a sun-dial, and Cathy could drowse under the sun (whilst Elspet probably turned from V*ogue*
to the *Tatler*) without lifting her wrist . . .

3

"Don't mind me, dear," said Mr. Weaver, "but you're
wanted."

Cathy sat up and in the same movement reached for
her vest. — Naturally all below-stairs knew their way up
to the roof. As Cook regretted, it was a great place for
canoodling. No one suspected Miss Pennon of canoodling, but all (below-stairs) knew she sun-bathed; Mr.
Weaver's sudden appearance was therefore less wizard-
like than it seemed; nor did he fail from his customary
tact.

"Miss McC. at the Castle has the same habit," he observed genially. "With a little more flesh round the mid-
riff you wouldn't be bad."

"What, Corky?" exclaimed Cathy, pausing in the act
of pulling on her dress.

"According to my confrère at Strathspey. Many a
time he's had to nip out with a bath-robe, the family
turning up unannounced. Speaking of which," added Mr.
Weaver, "have you a sister a Mrs. Maclaren?"

With regret Cathy detached her mind from the surprising apparition of her ex-instructress in the nude
(Why a bathrobe? Where *was* Corky, that she apparently hadn't a stitch with her?) to the almost equally
surprising but far less welcome apparition of an ex-sister.

It was indeed so long since she had given Muriel a thought, the term well enough described their relationship, at least on one side . . .

"Dear God!" groaned Cathy.

"Well, she's calling," said Mr. Weaver, rightly taking this as an affirmative and producing an oblong of pasteboard, "in white kid gloves no less. Complete with husband, female child and well-polished car of small British make."

"It would be."

"Also with a look in her eye expecting tea."

"Tell her I'm out," said Cathy.

"You don't want to see your nearest and dearest?"

"Would you?" asked Cathy reasonably.

"Certainly not *my* married sister," said Mr. Weaver, "for the reason she married a very accomplished forger. — In again, out again," sighed Mr. Weaver, "remind me after poker and I'll tell you how he once forged a cheque on the Poor Clergy Fund."

"He sounds a lot more interesting than *my* brother-in-law," envied Cathy.

"I never met a chap I liked more," agreed Mr. Weaver, "but one's got to protect oneself."

"Well, go along and protect me now," said Cathy. "Say I'm out. — And if you want a sixpenny bet, I bet you that card'll be left with a corner turned down."

4

"Miss Pennon it seems has gone with Miss Elspet to attend a gymkhana," regretted Mr. Weaver.

"Where?" asked Muriel eagerly.

"I believe at Chard, madam."

"That's twenty miles," said Archy.

170

"If not more, sir," agreed Weaver helpfully. "There is of course the possibility you might meet the horse-box returning; but Miss Pennon would be in the car with her ladyship and Miss Elspet."

Muriel's eye brightened.

"Mightn't we meet *them*?" she suggested.

"Depending on which route they take, to avoid traffic, certainly, madam. If in any case you care to leave your card —"

This was of course a solecism on Mr. Weaver's part; Muriel's card had been technically left already. But there was sixpence on it, and as though through absence of mind he extended it again.

Cathy won her bet. Bred on the Next-door Island, Muriel was possibly the last of her generation to turn down the corner of a visiting-card: in a minuscule way marking the end of an epoch.

31

MR. WEAVER, as has been seen, threw his mantle over Cathy as loyally as if she had been a true-born member of his own flock; but of course she wasn't. She stood out as neither ewe-lamb nor black sheep, but rather as goatling; and however accepted, and even popular, below-stairs, aroused there a good deal more curiosity than she ever guessed. Cook's definition of her as a lady, but déclassée, was generally accepted — especially since neither May nor Janice, and certainly not Bridie, knew what déclassée meant. Henry too acknowledged her a mem-sahib, if of some lesser breed without the law. ("The sort to go off with a sergeant," glossed Henry, "or even a railway-wallah.") "Anyway, her's a good sort," said May. "Her never breathed a morsel about that shoe — did her, Mr. Weaver?" " 'Tis nice to hear Shirley Temple ticked off," contributed Janice (so below-stairs, disrespectfully, referred to Elspet). "I often wish poor Miss Scott back amongst us, just for the pleasure!"

More or less a lady, definitely a good sort, and of course a first-class poker-player, so Cathy's image finally crystallized below-stairs, and few governesses have ever projected a better. There remained in addition one point upon which Mr. Weaver in particular frequently speculated.

"Would you say she was a virgin?" ruminated Mr. Weaver, untying his dressing-gown beside May's bed. (It was a measure of Cathy's standing that the pronoun traditionally reserved for the mistress of a house identified her at once.)

"I'd say more like a widow," offered May. "Goodness, Mr. Weaver, where's your pyjamas?"

"No wedding-ring," pointed out Mr. Weaver.

"Still bereaved," said May. "You can be bereaved without a wedding-ring — as my Bly aunt Milly well knows. If you're so interested, why not find out for yourself?"

"All in due course," said Mr. Weaver.

2

All in due course — Mr. Lutterel absent at Westminster, Lady Jean and Elspet absent at a wedding in Shropshire — Mr. Weaver himself carried up Cathy's dinner-tray. The additional circumstance that she had a heavy cold was rather an advantage; she was in bed already.

"With Cook's compliments, a nice cup of consommé," sympathized Mr. Weaver. "No need to put on a jacket, dear; just sit up a little and let me hand it you."

Over the rim of her soup-spoon Cathy regarded him warily; warily drank up Cook's consommé while Mr. Weaver casually loosened his tie. He wasn't in his dressing-gown. He was proceeding with some ceremony. But he knew how easily a moment might be let slip while a man got rid of his dickey. His boot-laces were loosened in advance; as Cathy finished her soup, Mr. Weaver undid a few essential buttons.

173

"You must think I'm desperate," said Cathy.

"Well, aren't you?" said Mr. Weaver.

"Not so desperate as all that," said Cathy.

"Ever since you came, I've seen something desperate about you," affirmed Mr. Weaver, taking the soup-bowl from her hands and setting it down out of harm's way. "But this you're going to like, dear; you're going to feel a new woman. Never mind about your heavy cold, I give you my word it'll be neither here nor there; just relax."

Like a great red sun his face stooped nearer and nearer. The smell of port on his breath was warming, almost stupefying. For a moment Cathy lay back passive as May or Janice, ready to be taken by a butler. Then she sat up again.

"May and Janice —"

"Good gracious, dear, you don't suppose I put you in the same category with *them?*" protested Mr. Weaver — one knee on the bed.

"— don't know anything about the sun," said Cathy incomprehensibly. "I dare say for them you do just as well. But not for me . . ."

She so sobbed, turning her face to the pillow, it was like hearing a child cry. Never would Mr. Weaver have thought it possible that with his boots already off he could have chucked in his hand so instantly. But he was truly fond of Cathy. He turned her pillow and tucked her in, and as soon as she was a little quieter, without rancour padded on along the corridor to May's room.

3

To the credit of both their mutual esteem moulted no feather. In fact in a curious way Mr. Weaver took over Muriel's rôle towards Cathy, at once protective and bracing: never letting her be caught napping like Miss Mc-Corquodale but reminding her in good time of all Lady Jean's engagements, seeing her present and correct for Sunday church, and particularly (basically) keeping her off the bottle.

Where else is the sun most reliably to be found? Cathy day by day tippled a little more; first a glass of port after lunch, then another with her supper, then over the poker-table two or three glasses more. "Heaven knows I'm no blue-ribbon myself," said Mr. Weaver, "also with Lutterel drinking less than a sparrow and corks not what they were I echo Cook on wilful waste. But aren't you tippling a bit much, dear?"

Cathy took the warning in good part. If rarely, towards evening, completely sober, she always got to bed under her own steam, and never failed at breakfast. Of course there were side-results; Cathy after making an effort to look bright at breakfast could hardly have heard Elspet spell cat. Elspet didn't mind. Elspet lived a fantasy-life of her own — now film-star, now bridesmaid to Royalty; and after poor conscientious Nanny Scott, found Cathy's absence of mind, and occasional physical absence on the roof, a happy change. Elspet covered up for her governess when necessary much as Mr. Weaver and Cook and Henry and Janice did for their leading poker-player . . .

32

"I'M SURE I don't know why I go on writing to Cathy," complained Muriel, "when she never answers."

"I don't either," said Archy practically.

Muriel sighed.

"It seems so awful having a sister one never sees . . ."

"It was far more awful having her in the house," reminded Archy. "If she wants to cut herself adrift, let her and be thankful."

Muriel sighed again. She had enjoyed writing "c/o Lady Jean Lutterel" on an envelope. But she saw her husband's point, also she had been genuinely hurt when Cathy didn't acknowledge even an enclosed very clever little sketch by Anna. Muriel stopped writing. Cathy didn't notice.

Alan had never written. Alan in the Midlands had his epistolary hands full keeping up a correspondence with Alice who'd removed to London, an Irish nurse who'd returned to Ireland, and another who'd emigrated to Australia — these last two amours blossoming inevitably from a spell in hospital after a cricket-ball cracked two of his ribs. Lightly injured male patients not uncommonly fall in love with their nurses; Alan characteristically fell in love with a couple, and as characteristically indited to both such fervent love-letters as could not fail to give a girl a lift whether in Dublin, Canberra, or the Edgware Road.

Now and again he communicated with the Maclarens too — once to give news of promotion, more commonly to explain why he couldn't be with them for Christmas or New Year or Easter or Whitsun. (To Alice succeeded Rosemary, to Rosemary Elizabeth; both locals.) But at least, as Muriel said, they were *in touch*; and she continued to think it a very sad thing to have a sister one never saw.

33

WHEN CATHY HAD been at the Manor five years Lady Jean raised her salary. — This was actually on the motion of Mr. Lutterel. Originally presented by his wife as being a man likely to argue about Matriculation, he had in fact taken no slightest part in Cathy's hiring; why he suddenly enquired what she was paid was because one of his constituents had a daughter very fond of little ones but also attracted to hair-dressing. "You must remember Cathy's *here* just as a friend," rather hedged Lady Jean; but the fifteen shillings came out at last. "Give her a hundred a year," said Mr. Lutterel briefly. "Good heavens, without a penny to spend she'll be richer than I am!" protested Lady Jean. But there were certain, admittedly few, junctures in her married life when she recognized her husband's authority, and that he should impose it on behalf of an attendant sprite, rather than to veto a little jaunt to Malta, was so fortunate, she ceded gracefully enough; and Cathy was to have a wonderful surprise.

Certainly Cathy was surprised. She also wondered. Where she failed was in gratitude.

"I'm glad I've given satisfaction," said Cathy — but scarcely on the right, grateful note.

"Good Cathy, but of course you have!" cried Lady

Jean. — She momentarily paused. Looking back over those five years, *had* Cathy given satisfaction? Elspet could certainly read; but otherwise at approaching twelve appeared scarcely more generally educated than at seven. ("Next year she must go to boarding-school," thought Lady Jean vaguely. "It's time she made more friends.") Nor did Cathy exactly shine, in her quality of attendant sprite. She was always about, at bazaar or fête, and had learned to bring a hamper; but less hovered (as an attendant sprite should) than tramped, at her employer's heels. Lady Jean had a very clear picture of herself being hovered over, and Cathy fell short of it; Miss Palmer from the Post Office was a born hoverer; so in his masculine way was Jimmy Trevennick; with Cathy at her heels Lady Jean sometimes felt not so much hovered over as dogged. There was also the point, or rather the suspicion, that Cathy got on too well with the staff. — One of the forces that turn nursery-governesses into attendant sprites is isolation. Nanny Scott, before Uncle Henry's providential legacy, Lady Jean had sometimes caught weeping from sheer loneliness. So had a previous sprite wept, a rather plain niece of Dr. James who unfortunately turned to social service. Recalling the defection of Nanny Scott and Helen James, Lady Jean felt herself a much-injured woman — and now here she was having to pay Cathy a hundred a year who really, Lady Jean by this time recognized, hadn't earned her keep at thirty. But she couldn't do without an attendant sprite of some sort, and when she contemplated all the nuisance of finding another —

"But of course you have!" repeated Lady Jean warmly. "Is it really five years we've been so happy together? It doesn't seem possible!"

Indeed when one looked at Cathy it didn't. In five years Lady Jean's beauty had so ripened (as in the early thirties true beauty does), she was even lovelier than at their first encounter. Elspet was passing from cherubic babyhood to angelic adolescence. The same five years had turned Mr. Lutterel grey as a badger and Weaver almost bald; Janice and May were grown blowsy, Henry showed signs of erysipelas. But there wasn't any change in Cathy. At twenty-eight she was just as light, stringy and desiccated as when she came; her rough red hair lustreless only from want of brushing, the few freckles on her nose more apparent only because she'd stopped using powder. It could hardly be said that she'd let herself go, for the reason that there was no prior standard of either beauty or amenity to let lapse. Only during her first half-year at the Manor did Cathy so much as attempt at amenity, and since, Lady Jean was quite right, hadn't even earned her keep.

The years that followed made not much more alteration in her. Lady Jean's beauty a little over-ripened, Elspet's bloomed; Cathy looked the same. If she'd taken to the bottle, it was but moderately; she didn't come out, like Henry, in grog-blossoms. A certain vagueness of manner, and unusual precision of speech, were sometimes noticeable towards the end of the day, but no more than could be excused as a slight eccentricity. — Elspet, returning term by term more sophisticated from a boarding-school patronized by royalty, made quite a thing of having an eccentric old governess. "Wait till you see my Cathy!" promised Elspet — inviting co-eval highborn sprigs back to gymkhana or point-to-point. "She's simply too eccentric to believe! Corky at the Castle's weird enough — but just wait till you see my Cathy!"

The British aristocracy have their faults. Disloyalty to a dependent is not one. However over-paid, however essentially useless, Cathy, like Corky, was kept on. Actually Miss McCorquodale was far more eccentric. Where Corky sunbathed, Cathy discovered, was on the shores of the loch. She stripped on the way down. "Hae ye e'er seen a suspender-belt," quoted Mr. Weaver, "hanging from a bonnie briar-bush?"

2

Old Mrs. Crosby at the dower-house died, and no successor was immediately found to replace her; but Jimmy Trevennick still tenanted the lodge. He was less of a fixture there than he had been; often a month or two passed without his putting in an appearance; once half a year. ("It's when the difference begins to tell," said Cook sagely. "Younger to begin with, and what's thirty to a man?" "Nearer thirty-five," said Mr. Weaver. "And her ladyship coming up to forty!" sighed Cook. "Time's a cruel thing, Mr. Weaver.") However a new sports car with Jimmy in it continued to roar up from time to time, and he was there in the drawing-room one Sunday afternoon when the League of International Friendship sent Herr Professor Schmidt.

34

HE WAS A small, hairy man, benevolent as a Christmas tree. Cathy entered to find him munching scones beside Lady Jean very comfortably, while Jimmy Trevennick strummed at the piano. As a picture of International Friendship it could hardly have been bettered.

"Here's Professor Schmidt!" said Lady Jean brightly. ("My attendant sprite," she added, to the Professor.) "Isn't it interesting, he collects folk-songs! He wants one that goes tooral-ay."

"Which don't?" said Jimmy Trevennick (thus explaining his situation at the key-board). "It's like tiddy-um-tum."

"Tiddy-um-tum?" repeated Professor Schmidt intelligently.

"Or tra-la-la."

There was a short, in the circumstances not unfamiliar pause. (The worst pause Cathy could remember was after a Dutch anthropologist's probe into the *droit de seigneur*.) Lady Jean made haste to fill it.

"But *this* one the Professor knows the *words* of," she explained hopefully. "Do repeat them, Professor!"

"Most willingly," beamed Herr Schmidt. "The immediate provenance, I may tell you, is from a prisoner-of-war camp commanded by my late uncle; but he as well as I suspected it to be of some antiquity. Here," added the Professor colloquially, "goes!

> Life's a pie with nothing in it,
>   Tooral-looral tooral-ay,
> Ain't we fools to want to cut it,
>   Tooral-looral tooral-ay?"

Again there was a slight pause, this time terminated, though not in words, by Cathy. With a gesture of extraordinary clumsiness, as she reached to take her own cup of tea she knocked the Professor's from his hand. — It had just been re-filled; Earl Grey and cream spilt sufficient to drench his knickerbockered knees. Lady Jean exclaimed, Jimmy Trevennick leapt to his feet with a crash on the treble and produced a handkerchief — only to collide with Mr. Weaver twitching a doyley from under a plate of paté sandwiches which flew in all directions and of which one skidded under the Professor's feet as he rose to be mopped up. It was in all such a scene of knockabout-comedy as the Manor rarely witnessed; but fortunately nice Herr Professor Schmidt took it all in good part.

2

The year following, as though he had been its herald, there was war again; the poor Germans being now well and strong.

Part Four

Part Four

35

BUT THIS WAS a new sort of war. — First a phoney war when nothing happened: in London theatres closing, then re-opening; from London a wave of mother-and-child evacuees first flooding out, then after a winter of bucolic discontent flooding back. Lady Jean however dispatched Elspet to a Strathspey connection at Washington, and Jimmy Trevennick rejoined his regiment.

Then a new sort of war again, as from Dunkirk a British army returned defeated — naturally to strike the foe afresh, but it was a pity they'd had to leave so much equipment behind. Pridefully nonetheless Admiral Duff boomed out "Eternal Father Strong to Save" at Sunday matins, and if he could would have referred also to the Royal Navy and amateur yachtsmen. "Land of Hope and Glory" was somewhat at a discount, the current favourite among the troops being rather "Roll Out the Barrel." "There'll Always Be an England," however ("And England Shall Be Free") was sung almost universally, as a defeated army straggled back across the Channel in the most beautiful summer weather of living memory.

Everything glittered. Never had the buttercup fields spread more golden. ("Like courage coming up all over England," said Miss Palmer unexpectedly; then blushed. "I mean, it's always easier to be brave when one's *warm*, don't you think?") Indeed the lavish sun encouraged; as day succeeded hot perfect day, the countryside fell almost into a basking mood. — Where Cathy basked was no longer on the leads but in the kitchen-garden; for years the Manor had made no more than a gesture at growing its own vegetables, so there was plenty to do in the way of hoeing and weeding — "Every *inch*, good Cathy!" instructed Lady Jean — before a new leaf could be turned; but Cathy also spent a good deal of time on her back in a derelict raspberry-cage. Raspberries meant jam, and home-made jam a sugar-allowance; reaching up to pull away handfuls of strangling bindweed, Cathy for once combined duty with self-indulgence. Not uncommonly her bare arms were pricked with blood-spots; now and then a little trickle of blood ran down to pit the soil between the bushes' roots. Cathy didn't notice, under the sun, in the spicy smell of bruised leaves; and once almost failed to notice the even pricklier threat of a hedgehog.

She had fortunately turned on her face, as the small snout thrust cautiously forth; the spines behind ready, but not yet erected. Cautiously, as though picking its way through a minefield, the small creature advanced, and halted. Cathy from a nose-to-nose distance of some fifteen inches regarded it warily. Was a hedgehog injurious to vegetables, or not? She couldn't remember. Botany at Miss Allen's hadn't included hedgehogs.

Should it be driven away with sticks and stones, or encouraged to stay and eat greenfly? As Weaver came tramping towards her across the humps of an old asparagus-bed —

"What do I do," called Cathy, "with a hedgehog?"

"Train it to stop a tank," said Mr. Weaver. "The French have packed in."

3

Eight thousand miles away in Ceylon, Tommy Bamber chucked up all his prospects to come home and fight for freedom. Actually he hadn't any prospects to speak of: risen to the position of manager of a tea-plantation he'd about reached his ceiling. But he had a very comfortable bungalow, and as a bachelor with a good income was as much run after, in Ceylon, as an eldest-son Guardee in London. He was also forty-two, and glumly recognized that his part in fighting for freedom would probably be both arduous and unheroic — at the best probably fire-watching at night after a day on the assembly-line in a factory. He nonetheless, unhesitatingly, came Home.

So from other parts of what had once been known as the Empire souls equally faithful and simple hurried to the defence of Nelson on his monument, Big Ben still sonorous above the House of Commons, and Eros in Piccadilly Circus. Faithful, brave and simple the great-grandchildren of the Empire-builders flocked Home — and not infrequently before re-embarkation (not all were Tommy's ripe age), encountered Olive and Sylvia.

Both Jacko's tenants, if now a bit long in the tooth, gallantly worked overtime. So did Jacko work overtime: many a week when the laundry didn't come Jacko washed sheets himself and draped them to dry out of an upstairs window. For the further encouragement of Olive's and Sylvia's friends, as the bombs began to drop he rigged up a very nice little air-raid shelter in the base-ment — religious pictures alternating with pin-ups all round the sand-bagged walls, and whisky practically free at half-a-crown a doctored nip. He also acquired himself a Warden's tin hat with a W on the front. No one quite knew how he came by it, his enemies said off a corpse, but Jacko was undoubtedly once or twice seen chucking sand on an expended incendiary, and it was no time to split hairs.

4

Somewhere near Chard, Captain Powell (R.N. rtd.) and Sir Rowland March, K.C.B., leant on their spades and took an easy. Both were over seventy, but the Home Guard knew no age limit, and they were engaged along with several other contemporaries in digging a section of the ditch designed to run from the Bristol Channel to Lyme Bay and halt panzer-brigades in case of invasion. It was about three feet deep and six wide.

"Not that they'll ever get here," said Captain Powell cheerily.

The Governor said nothing. He suspected that much of the general optimism (they were all very cheery) was due to the unaccustomed extrusion of sweat from open pores. But it was not a time to be realistic, so he said nothing. — Captain Powell glanced at him uneasily, vaguely recalling something fishy about the old boy: not precisely a court-martial, some sort of blot on his official copy-book. Nurtured as he was in the Nelson tradition, the Captain's mind instinctively turned to flogging: and if it was true that the Governor had had two Fuzzy-Wuzzies flogged to death, Captain Powell, whose opinions moved slowly but doggedly with the times, was almost prepared to suspect him of defeatism as well as inhumanity.

Like Cathy his pupil, the Governor was always slightly out of step.

He was out of step in another sense. He alone of that ditch-digging squad had no one belonging to him engaged on more active service. (In fact the Governor had no one much belonging to him at all.) It was true that in this Second World War elders no longer spoke of giving their young, to their country; but they spoke of them, with pride, and, unspokenly, feared for them; and from this common bond of pride and apprehension the Governor was necessarily excluded.

To the credit of Captain Powell, he even during the First World War had refused the current canting phrase when a son was blown up with his ship off Gallipoli. But then Powells were always Service.

5

Muriel enjoyed double cause for pride. Heedless of his father's injunction (by this time indeed passed completely from his memory), Alan had joined up at once and Anna was in the A.T.S. A long silence was broken as Muriel wrote to give Cathy the tidings — adding loyally that Archy brought home work every single night. "As for me, I'm just W.V.S." wrote Muriel, "but what I've done as well is to organize an Old Girls fire-watching squad to fire-watch on Miss Allen's roof. Of course it isn't Miss Allen's any more, it changed hands long ago — but it's still our dear old school! ! Judith Bamber's in,

*and lots of others you probably won't remember, and I
must say that apart from everything else it's pulled the
Old Girls' Association together enormously, which was
getting rather slack. What are you doing, Cathy?"*

It was this last phrase that prevented Cathy answering
immediately. She fully intended to answer; only delayed
until she had something more positive and heroic to report than kitchen-gardening, even if it was but going
into munitions like Janice and May. — Janice and May
had gone back into munitions as instantly as Bridie had
gone back to Ireland; the operative word perhaps "back."
All three returned to a way of life already experienced,
familiar in its rewards, of high pay and canteens or
safety and decent butter, as with its penalties of night-
shifts or heavy-handed Da. Cathy faced the unknown,
and after ten years as a fainéant attendant sprite no sort
of radical change came easily; but spurred by Muriel's
letter (which was in fact just what Muriel had hoped
would be its effect), Cathy more and more girded up her
loins, braced her sinews, and mentally prepared the
phrase in which she would give her employer notice.
That she didn't do so immediately was because she'd
been an attendant sprite for ten years and Lady Jean had
blue rings under her eyes; but especially as the raids on
London increased in number and destructiveness, Cathy's
resolve hardened to join the A.T.S. like Anna and write
back to Muriel from a gun-site.

36

WELLSCOMBE ALWAYS knew when there'd been another raid on London because the morning papers didn't arrive.

"Which at least makes one get on with one's job!" said Lady Jean brightly. "I'm going straight to the drawing-room to sort gramophone-records for the Red Cross!"

Cathy, in fact much as usual, went straight out to the kitchen-garden. (It would have been scarcely an exaggeration to write and tell Muriel she was on the land, only Cathy knew in her heart it wouldn't wash, from an address still c/o Lady Jean Lutterel.) She was in the kitchen-garden from nine o'clock till noon, when she would normally have returned, like any other outdoor-worker, by a back-entry. Only because the weather was still so fine, and her shoes consequently unmuddied, did she make directly for the great door into the hall, there to find Weaver at the telephone with the receiver in his hand and on his face an expression of peculiar blankness.

"Thank God," said Weaver softly. "Here's one *you'd* better take . . ."

For a moment Cathy could only look blankly back. No papers had come that morning; and Mr. Lutterel was at Westminster.

"Who is it?" asked Cathy nervously.

Pushing the receiver into her hand —

"Says she's Mrs. Trevennick, dear," muttered Weaver.

2

The voice at the other end of the line was high, light, and curiously artificial.

"*Now* who am I speaking to?" it demanded impatiently.

"Miss Pennon," said Cathy — hearing her own voice, under the shock, artificial too. "Lady Jean's," she added ridiculously, "attendant sprite."

"Of course," agreed the voice. "Jimmy told me. *I'm* Mrs. Trevennick."

"Weaver told me," echoed Cathy.

"Weaver?"

"The butler."

"Jimmy's mother," said the voice. "I'm Jimmy's mother. He's been killed, you see. At Calais. It's official. Some one should break it to her."

"Mr. Lutterel —" began Cathy foolishly; intending to say Mr. Lutterel wasn't there; then checked herself. At the other end of the line Jimmy's mother either laughed or cried.

"*Not* her husband. *You* break it," said Mrs. Trevennick. "That's all."

3

"And might have been a good deal worse," observed Mr. Weaver, uncupping his hand from his ear. "To be frank, dear, I momentarily fancied he'd betrayed her affections and wedded another."

"You never liked him, did you?" said Cathy.

194

"To be frank again, I found him too damned affable," said Mr. Weaver. "*Your* life's not going to be blighted, I hope?"

"Not mine," said Cathy.

Mr. Weaver, following her glance towards the shut drawing-room door, sighed not so much in compassion as relief.

"Anyway, it's up to you not me, dear. A woman's touch, a woman's care . . . One ring and I'll be in with the brandy," he added, "unless you'd like a nip yourself first?"

But Cathy refused. She by this time knew herself well enough to be aware that alcohol loosened her self-control, and it wasn't she who was now licenced to weep. Indeed, what she would have wept for — like Weaver having always found Jimmy Trevennick too damned affable — was simply the untimely cutting-off of a sprig of the world's beauty. (May and Janice, subsequently in tears for days, though they didn't know it shared the same feeling.) Cathy opened the door stone cold sober.

4

Her employer, to sort gramophone-records, had seated herself on the floor. It is a posture in which few women of forty can appear graceful: Lady Jean, leaning forward from the waist above crossed knees, might have been a dancer performing some complicated but easy exercise. During the past few months she was become less slender than thin; but now so convoluted appeared simply pliant as a willow-wreath. (*And all round my hat I'll wear a green willow.*) Upon Cathy's entrance she looked up amusedly.

"What I've *found!*" cried Lady Jean. "Good Cathy, do

you remember the Tango? No, of course you don't; you wouldn't learn it. All *these* are to go to the Red Cross; or else for salvage; they can decide for themselves."

"I have something dreadful to tell you," said Cathy.

Instantly the willow-wand back straightened. No papers had come, and Mr. Lutterel was at Westminster . . .

"Jimmy?"

Cathy nodded.

"His mother's just telephoned . . ."

With the same artificiality that had informed Mrs. Trevennick's voice, but now translated into motion, Lady Jean delicately fitted a record into its sleeve.

"Missing?"

"No; dead," said Cathy. "She asked me to break it to you. If I've done it badly, I ask your pardon."

She was in fact asking pardon for much more; for her mimicry at the poker-table, for her renegading to the natives. But nothing of this could be expressed, or indeed mattered, at such a moment; certainly not to her employer. The worst of it was that Lady Jean didn't weep at all. The sea-blue eyes merely widened; focussed upon some point beyond Cathy's shoulder; then darkened to holes in a blank mask.

"Thank you, now please will you go away?" said Lady Jean politely. "And as Mr. Lutterel isn't here, tell Cook not to bother about lunch."

All afternoon, far into the evening, from behind the shut drawing-room door echoed the strains of a Viennese waltz. Cathy hovered outside fending off first Weaver with tea, then Cook blubbering into a cup of consommé, then Weaver again with brandy. It was late, almost nine, before Lady Jean at last emerged; but she must have thought it much later.

"Still up, good Cathy?" asked Lady Jean vaguely.

"I left my gloves on the Bible-box," lied Cathy.

"Which always brings bad luck," said Lady Jean. "Good night to you . . ."

On the landing, opposite the dim mirror between the tapestries of Spring and Summer, Cathy saw her pause a moment. The reflected face was still beautiful, only now expressionless. It seemed to practise an expressionless, or rather careful, unbetraying smile; and so smiling, Lady Jean went on to her room.

5

To Mr. Lutterel returning next day his wife suddenly announced her intention of going up to London to drive an ambulance. A duke's daughter, she had no more doubt of being able to commandeer an ambulance than of being able, in other circumstances, to commandeer a yacht; and as she pointed out, hadn't she driven the runabout for years?

"And if I should say," suggested Mr. Lutterel, "that I'd rather you didn't unnecessarily risk your life?"

"Darling, I should simply blow my brains out!" said Lady Jean lightly. "I'm so *bored*, doing nothing here in Devon!"

She had her way, of course. As she pointed out again, wasn't there a spare bed for her in Mr. Lutterel's Westminster flat? — "Unless I should be inconveniencing you?" added Lady Jean, more brightly still. "I wouldn't want you to turn out any pretty little secretary!"

Her husband looked at her thoughtfully. He had married her for her beauty. Why she had married him, he even on their wedding-day had recognized to be because after three Seasons marked by a peculiar shortage of eldest sons (the First World War having taken its toll) it was time for her to marry, and he had the Lutterel name and place to offer, also as a rising M.P. the chance of making her wife to a Cabinet Minister. (At least; Lady Jean possibly visualized herself in Downing Street.) But the hard-working years had slipped by without promotion, and the fact that Mr. Lutterel's majority was always safe made him if anything rather overlooked. — All this passing through his mind, he forgave even, along with all the rest, his lady-wife's moment of vulgarity.

They were standing by the hearth in the hall. Under the marble cherubim a small fire slightly flickered. Thrusting the logs together with his foot —

"And the house?" asked Mr. Lutterel.

"One thing I won't have is evacuees," said Lady Jean firmly. "They'd bring bugs and be terribly unhappy. Besides, we'll want it ourselves, at week-ends. We'll just leave Cathy in charge."

37

IN A WAY it was hard, in a way it was easier, to accept frustration instead of change. "Good Cathy, of *course* you want to help the war effort!" cried Lady Jean. "But how can you do it better than here, keeping the house open? I mean, just *look* at Mr. Lutterel! Without the house to get back to at week-ends he'd simply *collapse!*"

The house, and the House, thought Cathy: the one home of the Lutterels since Doomsday, the other the House of Commons. Mr. Lutterel belonged blood and bone to both. Looking at him across the breakfast-table as her employer directed — but covertly, for she felt he didn't want to be looked at — Cathy saw him indeed much worn. His long nose was fleshless as a bird's beak; each furrow from nostril to mouth as explicit of stress as the rings round his wife's eyes. For an appalled moment, looking at Mr. Lutterel, the thought crossed Cathy's mind that England mightn't win the war . . .

No papers had come. He hadn't his usual screen of *The Times* to put up. He looked back at Cathy gravely.

"I should be obliged," said Mr. Lutterel.

She stayed.

It wasn't anything to write to Muriel about. She wasn't even properly on the land. As a contribution to the food supply, however, Cathy grew and salted down a really massive quantity of runner-beans. Runner-beans are grown so easily, she was able to salt down crock after crock without interrupting the current supply of fresh. At any week-end, as indeed all through the week itself, runner-beans never lacked. "Good Cathy, how clever you are!" congratulated Lady Jean. "Didn't I always say you were a treasure? One day I believe you'll even grow a *lettuce!*"

Lettuces were another matter. Cathy had sown some and they'd come up, but to attain any proper heart or shapeliness lettuces need to be tied round, and with no more than a hedgehog for under-gardener Cathy tended to let them run to seed; productive only of large coarse leaves Cook refused to dignify with her vinaigrette sauce . . .

So did the Manor run to seed. In the wake of May and Janice defected Henry, who'd at least occasionally clipped the laurels, into Army Catering. ("Heaven help all *he* serves by sea or land," observed Mr. Weaver.) Only Cathy and Mr. Weaver and Cook were left to perform the basic offices of opening windows to air rooms and keeping alight a fire under the marble cherubim.

"Which I for one see no point in," said Cook. "I shouldn't wonder if before we're through we're using wood in the boiler."

Cathy and Mr. Weaver exchanged glances. They shared a common superstition neither ever mentioned.

"Good gracious," said Mr. Weaver, "there's fuel from the timber here to last till Doomsday."

"And who's to saw and fetch it?" snapped Cook.

"I, with these lily-white hands," said Mr. Weaver.

Between them Cook and Cathy dissuaded him from using a ladder; he tackled only lower branches, within reach from the ground, so that in due course the woods behind the Manor began to show the sort of browsing-line from which is deducible whether a proprietor runs cattle, ornamental deer, or goats. What could have been deduced at Wellscombe was an elderly but resolute butler.

3

"Take my deal, dear," said Mr. Weaver, "I'm all over this perishing Elastoplast."

Cathy dealt without enthusiasm. There was no more poker. The only game played below-stairs was now three-handed whist — Cook absolutely refusing to learn, and indeed probably incapable of learning, bridge.

"Shirley Temple didn't I suppose leave any tiddly-winks behind?" asked Mr. Weaver bitterly.

"If you mean Elspet, no," said Cathy. "I don't know what's the fashion in Washington, but whatever it is (hearts for trumps, Cook; try and remember) you can bet she's either very good or very bad at it."

"Bad," said Mr. Weaver intelligently. "Millionaires patting her hand to console . . ."

"Such a beautiful young lady as she must be, why shouldn't they?" asked Cook.

"Exactly," said Cathy. "It isn't your lead."

"There should be some sort of international million-aires' warning-service," mused Mr. Weaver.

"Wi' eyelashes lang as her ain pedigree," said Cathy —
briefly falling back into mimicry — "would it no' be
better to warn Hollywood?"

"If no one else is going to lead, I am," said Cook, laying down the ace of hearts.

They were foolish games, games quite unworthy of
Cathy's and Mr. Weaver's skill, played in the huge idle
kitchen. Cathy, dealing first for herself, then for Weaver,
then watching Cook poke out the cards one by one,
often recalled Jacko's dashing expert way with an equally
thumb-worn pack.

4

Jacko died rather heroically. He didn't intend to. It just
so happened that one morning when the sirens sounded
over Soho Sylvia was upstairs in bed having a long lie.
Jacko, as he nipped downstairs to the shelter, unhesitatingly made the kind decision to let her sleep her sleep
out. She slept like a log; probably wouldn't even hear the
racket. As usual on such occasions he put on his Warden's hat (it always looked better, after a raid, to be seen
so accoutred), took a glass of whisky, invoked his mother
and St. Patrick, and settled down to check his various
bank-accounts.

He then remembered that Sylvia, announcing her intention of taking a long lie, had also announced the intention of subsequently washing her hair. For all Jacko's
warnings, she did it in petrol. (And where she got that
petrol, with rationing so strict, Jacko often asked himself.
He suspected, and it hurt him, some underhand tie-up
with the manager of a local garage.) Thus there was
quite possibly a can of petrol standing about somewhere

on his top storey, a thing which in a raid no responsible householder likes.

Jacko had five thousand in the Westminster, another five in Lloyds, and in Barclays seven. It was also through Barclays that he'd lent the Government two thousand free of interest as a defence in case jumped on for tax-evasion. Such figures never failed to hearten, nor did they now; only as the bombs began to drop definitely upon Soho, Sylvia's can of petrol worried him.

He nipped upstairs again at exactly the moment when the bomb hit. — Before him as behind brick and plaster collapsed into rubble; the sharp blue flame of petrol swallowed up in a greater conflagration. Jacko just might, just possibly, have saved himself by batting down and out under his Warden's tin hat but that Sylvia was suddenly clinging round his neck. He couldn't abandon her, she had a grip like a vise; thus they were discovered next day charred to cinders together, and Jacko had died heroically.

It fell to the painful lot of Olive (fortunately out on duty at the time) to identify them. She organized a splendid funeral. All Soho came. Jacko's rough friends weighed in with a four-foot wreath, also acted as bearers. Even the police, who'd at least known where they were with Jacko, sympathetically routed the cortège past new bomb-craters to St. Patrick's Soho Square; and over his coffin, just as he'd have wished, was spread a Union Jack.

Olive had gone to great pains to procure one large enough. Union Jacks abounded, but only of a size to be flown on a stick thrust into a rubble-heap, or hung by the fly over a fish-and-chip stall. — Several retired admirals, including Admiral Duff, were at this juncture writing

letters to *The Times* in protest against Jacks flown by
the fly; but then they none of them kept fish-and-chip
stalls in the Blitz.

5

The flat in Westminster on that same morning had but
its windows blown in; it was however a well-known fact
that window-panes of quite normal size fragmented into
enough broken glass to build a green-house, and those at
the flat reached from floor to ceiling. Splinters crackled
underfoot like a frozen fall of snow, there was glass on
and in the beds, glass in the bath, everything sparkled
with glass even to a loaf on the table laid for breakfast
which sparkled like a wedding-cake . . .

Lady Jean returned from duty to find her husband,
who had slept in his bed, smelling strongly of Chanel
No. 5 as he attempted to put her dressing-table to rights.
Pausing and sniffing —

"Darling, not the last of my Chanel!" wailed Lady
Jean.

"I'm afraid so," apologized Mr. Lutterel.

"Then Elspet must send me some from Washington,"
said Lady Jean crossly, and pulling off a smoke-grimed
tin hat, "or what's the good of having a cousin in the
Diplomatic who can't even get America into the war?"

"You might go across yourself and strengthen his
hand," suggested Mr. Lutterel.

"Darling, I'd be simply too bored, in Washington,"
said Lady Jean. "At least there's always something going
on —" (by which she meant blood, toil and sweat, also
the possibility of sudden death) — "in London!"

Such being her mood, and Mr. Lutterel strict in his

attendance at the House, week-ends at the Manor became more and more rare. Bombed railways made the transit hazardous in any case, also the return to the metropolis, after forty-eight hours' comparative security, taxed nerves already over-strained. The Lutterels stayed in Town.

38

NATURALLY THE NEWS got back to Harrods. Meeting her friend Mrs. Anstruther in the Groceries —

"I hear dear Jean's driving an ambulance!" shouted Lady Maud.

"Don't bawl so," said Mrs. Anstruther irritably. "I may be going blind, but I'm not deaf. What did you say?"

"I said Jean's driving an ambulance," repeated Lady Maud, thinking how doddery poor Amy was getting, "in the Blitz."

"Making herself conspicuous as usual," said Mrs. Anstruther, noticing that poor Maud now had to use a stick. "Why can't she stay at home and look after her husband?"

"That's a very unkind thing to say," rebuked Lady Jean's aunt. "And she *is* looking after him. She's come up to the flat in Westminster. According to Kate Elliot in the same block, she frequently boils him a breakfast egg."

"Where does she get it?" demanded Mrs. Anstruther jealously.

"Strathspey," said Lady Maud — lowering her voice

as though disclosing an illicit source of opium. "The difficulty's containers."

"Tea-caddies," said Mrs. Anstruther, "padded with *The Times*. If *I* sent up a tea-caddy, and *you* dropped a line —"

"Maybe," said Lady Maud.

"Anyway, come and have lunch with me," invited Mrs. Anstruther. "You choose where."

"Claridges," said Lady Maud.

39

QUIETLY PASSED THE months at Wellscombe;
a year passed. Weaver took longer and longer to
cut and bring in fuel, until it became almost his
sole activity: when Mr. Lutterel and Lady Jean appeared
to have stopped coming down for good he gave all silver
a final polish and consigned it to green baize. Cook's
standards fell to the level of fish-pie, and in the evenings
she declared even whist beyond her. Cathy and Mr.
Weaver attempted first bézique, then settled for chess;
very long, slow games during which the latter frequently
drowsed between moves. — So indeed did Cathy, ending
each unheroic day equally dog-tired. Whatever was done
in the Manor to keep it aired, fairly clean, a little alive,
was done by her single-handed; even the hedgehog having vanished from the kitchen-garden.

She achieved a second crop of runner-beans, however,
just as the last salted-down crock emptied, and the raspberry-canes produced fruit for a little more jam. (Three
pots as against two; which Cook sent up to Westminster;
and which were smashed on the way, but it didn't matter because Lady Jean, along with a fresh supply of
Chanel No. 5 had had some specially vitamin-reinforced
jam from Washington.) To Cathy, who had always de-

tested housework, the hours spent in the kitchen-garden, especially if there was any sun, were the best of the day.

It was there that she suddenly observed striding towards her a young woman in the uniform of the A.T.S.

"You're my Aunt Cathy, I'm your niece Anna," said the young woman. "You've changed."

2

Cathy stared at her. She was Muriel's daughter all right: fresh-complexioned, big-busted, confident, and, obviously, conscientious. (A sergeant's three stripes on her sleeve.)

"But you can't possibly remember me," said Cathy. "You were only about four."

"I did ask an old man at the house," admitted Anna, "if you were still here; but of course I remember you. You once nearly pushed me out of a window. I can remember a bright red sky, and you standing behind me, and then your hand on my back and suddenly everything feeling tremendously exciting and dangerous. It's given me the best Earliest Memory on our gun-site. None of the others remember anything worse than being left in a pram outside a pub. — You've changed," accused Anna.

"Well, it's nearly twenty years," said Cathy reasonably. "I'm going grey." She still knew it wasn't any physical change that disappointed Anna, but rather a change in personality, from the dangerous to the domestic, the kitchen-gardening; as her niece's next words proved.

"Peggy particularly wanted to meet you," said Anna sombrely. "It's Peggy who's driving the lorry. But by now I expect she's watching her time-sheet . . . Good heavens, Aunt Cathy," cried Anna, abruptly turning to look back across the bean-rows at the Manor chimneys, "haven't you even evacuees, in that huge house?"

"The Lutterels come down at week-ends," said Cathy. "How's your mother?"

"Splendid," said Anna. "One night when Judith Bamber had flu she put out three incendiaries all by herself. And Daddy works eighteen hours a day and Uncle Alan's been taken prisoner in Libya," resumed Anna rapidly, her eye still jealous, so to speak, of Unoccupied Premises. "Good heavens, Aunt Cathy, just two people at week-ends can't take up much room! Mother would have had it full of Poles. She's always remembered how huge it was."

"Of course, she came here," recalled Cathy.

"We all did," said Anna, "but you were away at a gymkhana. The butler told us." — For the first time her youthful, her sergeant's, severity relaxed; she grinned. "Daddy drew me a wonderful picture of him and we cut it out and made it bow from the waist."

"Very amusing," said Cathy.

"That's what mother said," agreed Anna. "You sounded just like her . . ."

Cathy swallowed the affront. — How indeed explain the difference between Muriel's snobbish esteem for any butler whatsoever, and that of an attendant sprite for a butler who in the first place hadn't raped her and whose hands were now so unbutlerishly scarred? No communication was possible, between Cathy and her niece standing together in the bean-rows; as each, if on different grounds, recognized.

"Good-bye, Aunt Cathy," said Anna politely. "I expect Peggy's having kittens . . ."

"A very firm young party," said Mr. Weaver.

"My niece Anna," said Cathy.

"Took me for a peasant," said Mr. Weaver, reaching into his trouser-pocket. "Half-a-crown, no less."

"I wonder you demeaned yourself," said Cook.

"Times change," said Mr. Weaver. "I'll put it to my War Savings."

The weekly visit from Miss Palmer to exact contributions to this particular form of war-effort was in fact the Manor's chief link with the outside world. Miss Palmer was pointedly discreet in taking each member of a household aside to lick stamps in privacy: though now retired, she had spent so many years combating a village postmistress's reputation for not being discreet, even husbands and wives on her round were similarly protected. So they none of them at the Manor, though so small and enclosed a society, knew what the others put in. Cathy herself put in thirty shillings. She had almost no expenses, and barely used her clothing-coupons. She saved at least six pounds a month.

The months passed, the years passed. America came in. Elspet in Washington not only married a millionaire but divorced him on the plea of mental cruelty, thus acquiring an income larger than her father's. It quite desolated Lady Jean that she wasn't at the wedding, but war was war.

The tide of war turned: then lapped again with such increasing force, Alan after two years in an Italian prison-camp found himself at liberty simply to walk out with the aim of rejoining any Allied unit advancing up the peninsula. If the Eyeties had packed up, however, the Germans hadn't; like many another eager compatriot, Alan found himself at liberty, but on the run.

40

STUMBLING DOWN THROUGH the chestnut-wood he fell heavily, hauled himself up, hobbled on, and so came upon the ghost of a summer-house. What had been its original frivolous shape — Swiss châlet, rustic cot, even pagoda? — was impossible to guess, most of the timber having been stripped for firewood; only its situation, commanding so extensive and beautiful a view, suggested summer-house rather than pig-stye. But a low substructure of brick remained, heaped against, where the floor-boards had been ripped up, with an accumulation of leaf-mould. Alan crept in, and lost consciousness.

2

When he awoke it was still, or again, day. At any rate he could see. He saw first, level with his eyes, a snail-shell; then a twig; then a foot in a rough countrywoman's espadrille.

Not only rough, but patched. The thongs were part leather and part string; knotted finally, however, about an ankle of unbucolic narrowness. With an effort Alan raised his eyes to a hem; of broadcloth, the sort of cloth made into English riding-habits; and it was indeed in

English (though much accented) that his discoverer addressed him.

"I am the Marchesa San Filipe," she said. "You are on my husband's land. I regret, but I must ask you to go away at once."

Carefully, Alan hauled himself up. It seemed that no bones had been broken, on his long downhill run; he could stand. But not much more; as his knee buckled he had to brace himself against the brick.

"I regret," repeated the Marchesa, "but my husband is extremely pro-German."

"Who are running," suggested Alan — all too aware that he was on the run himself.

"He is also a man of honour," said the Marchesa. "Had our allies been advancing, it would be different. To take you in now he would feel sucking-up."

"At least let me compliment you," said Alan wryly, "on your idiomatic English."

The Marchesa fleetingly smiled.

"When I was very young, I was educated at an English school . . ."

"Corky's, by God!" cried Alan.

Even the effort to get on his feet had been too much for him. The pair of ancient but armed retainers (lurking ready if needful to shoot and bury him) had to carry the Marchesa's old schoolfellow up bodily to the Villa San Filipe.

3

He recovered consciousness again in a great high room furnished in Art Nouveau. The key-note was fumed oak, shallowly carved with water-lilies: a suite imported from Maples in 1910. But there was nothing Art Nouveau

214

about the Marchese, the Marchesa's husband; in any British reference he was a Landseer, a gaunt old stag still monarch of his glen. (He was much older than his wife who had been the Baroness; probably on the wrong side of seventy.) She spoke rapidly to him in Italian, then almost immediately, from courtesy, switched to English; but Alan was beyond comprehending. He lay passive on the Maples settee; rousing only once, as in scuttled a ragged serving-maid bearing a pair of lamb's-wool slippers, to kneel and unknot the thongs of her mistress's espadrilles.

"*I must learn to tie a bow!*" giggled the Baroness. "But I never have, have I, Enrico?"

4

It was actually a point to which the Marchese returned more than once in subsequent conversation. Evidently the tale of his wife's weekly incarceration had passed into family legend.

"What I have never understood," he meditated, "is why the Marchesa — or, as she was then, the Baroness — should have been required to tie her own shoes. Was there not a servant to tie them?"

"Teresa!" exclaimed Alan and the Marchesa together.

"Exactly," said the Marchese. "I am all the more at a loss."

Summoning the spirit of Corky to his aid —

"Well, I suppose it was the principle of the thing," said Alan. "Just as at Eton a fag whose father may be a Duke learns to make toast."

"Manners and Self-reliance!" put in the Marchesa joyously.

"Ah! You were at Eton?" nodded the Marchese, looking encouraged.

"Not exactly," admitted Alan. "But at a school for Sons of Gentlemen." (At last, in however unexpected circumstances, brassplate and letter-head paid off; the Marchese again nodded appreciatively.) "Where if I didn't make toast," added Alan, "I used to Blanco a senior prefect's cricket-pads. What I mean is, it's the principle of the thing."

"I have never learned even to make toast!" giggled the Baroness.

5

Middle-aged as she now was, shod in patched espadrilles, caught up in the tail-end of her country's defeat and as uncertain of her future as of which side she really wanted to win, the Baroness — for so Alan continued to think of her — could still giggle. Her innate frivolousness equated almost, in the circumstances, to Keats's cardinal virtue of Negative Capability: the Baroness was capable of being in any number of uncertainties, and doubts, without any irritable reaching after fact and reason. She lived morally, so to speak, hand to mouth. — To Alan, for example, she confessed herself so strongly pro-British, only loyalty to her husband had prevented her helping local partisans derail a German troop-train ("They rolled down great boulders!" recalled the Baroness enviously. "All their faces blacked!") but when he asked what she'd done with Germans actually billeted in the Villa, replied ingenuously that she'd arranged little lieder-concerts . . .

"There was an *Oberst* — what would you call him, a

Colonel? — who sang Brahms quite beautifully," explained the Baroness, "and as I play the piano a little myself I could accompany him. — Poor Freidrich, I wonder where he is now? You would have liked him so much!"

Alan felt a pang of jealousy all the more irrational since he felt no jealousy of the Marchese. This had perhaps something to do with the circumstance that the Marchese didn't resort to his wife's room, but slept apart in a narrow, cell-like chamber of his own. Alan in fact had come to share, couldn't help sharing, the Baroness's obvious respect, and almost her affection, for her old Landseer stag . . .

"My husband, you will have realized, is much older than I," explained the Baroness. "More than sixty when we married! — I am of course his second wife."

"Any children?" asked Alan awkwardly.

"Two. Two sons — not by me, by the Principessa Anna-Beatrice (actually a connection of mine) he married first," said the Baroness, "both killed fighting with the Tedescos. So he is very gallant, *nicht wahr?*" She paused, evidently throwing her mind back in search of the exact phrase. "He keeps, does he not, a stiff upper lip?"

At which moment, as it happened, the Marchese stalked in from the daily round of his shell-pocked fields. Alan's knee still made the act of rising, and particularly of standing, extremely painful; but he hauled himself up nonetheless and stood until his host was seated.

In general however the Marchese left his wife and his guest much to themselves. It delighted him, he observed courteously, that the Marchesa should have a little fresh company, a little distraction, in her hard disrupted life; he was especially pleased that the hazards of war should have reunited her with an old schoolfellow. "You will have much to talk about," prompted the Marchese. "There is nothing so agreeable as reviving memories of one's youth . . ."

If Alan felt briefly that he was being put on his honour, the long ensuing conversations, in the Art Nouveau saloon, or, later, on the terrace, were just as delightful as the Marchese foresaw. — It was noticeable that the Baroness's revived memories related entirely to herself and Alan. She never once asked news of Muriel or Cathy, equally her old schoolfellows; nor did Alan introduce them into the gentle idyll that to the sound of retreating gunfire so pleasantly and naturally unfolded.

6

"Did you ever see me," asked Alan, "waiting outside while you were kept in?"

"Indeed I did!" giggled the Baroness. "Such a little boy, beside old Teresa! She used to call you my little lover!"

"What Corky would have called putting ideas into your head," said Alan, lightly.

The Baroness giggled again.

"They were there already, my dear. You must remember I was already nine! Of course I noticed you! But why did you never wait till I came out?"

"I was probably too frightened of old Teresa," said Alan.

"It was her duty to frighten you," explained the Baroness, only half-humorously. "Even a little boy of six, it was her duty to frighten. Poor Teresa — *la poverina!* — do you know that when my family left the Island, and she was too old to take with us, she hanged herself? — Oh, my dear Alan," cried the Baroness, almost in the same breath, "do you remember the Governor's ball?"

"Of course I do. You went as a Powder-puff," said Alan — feeling swansdown against his bare knees.

"You danced the polka with me!"

"You remember *that?*" marvelled Alan.

"A woman always remembers her first ball," sighed the Baroness. "Also you were my first partner!"

"Later on I couldn't get near you," reminded Alan. "There were too many older chaps ahead."

The Baroness looked complacent.

"I have always had a success, at balls. In fact it was at a ball in Rome that my dear Enrico was first attracted to me."

—And how did *he* get ahead, wondered Alan, of so many younger chaps? Through wealth, prestige, or family connections? In any case the Baroness appeared to have no regrets, even as she re-lived that Roman triumph . . .

"Of course I was a blonde," she recalled, "which in Italy gives one an advantage. I still had rivals," she added fairly. "My own cousin Pauline, with a really splendid bust . . . But how she *pushed* it!" giggled the Baroness. "Like two melons on a plate! — Oh, my dear Alan, do you remember the Wood-nymph?"

In Alan's ears suddenly re-echoed the scandal of the Governor's ball.

"Who *showed too much?*"

"It was a lesson to me," said the Baroness seriously.

"Even then, though I was so stupid at school, I had my wits. *Never* more than the discreetest décolletage!"

"But swansdowny?" suggested Alan.

"Well, yes; swansdowny!" agreed the Baroness.

(She still had a taste for swansdown. In the salotto, in the evening, she sometimes wore a little jacket of faded silk with swansdown round the collar. Alan was tempted to put out a finger to it; but because he was on his honour, refrained.)

"How long ago it all seems!" sighed the Baroness.

Alan sighed reciprocally. Sometimes they didn't talk at all, they just sat on the terrace and sighed. When Alan could hobble again they sighed in the old ruined summer-house, the scene of their first re-encounter; and there it was that they at last kissed.

7

The evening was so still, the Italian air so mild, the Baroness had ventured forth in that same little jacket. More than mild was the Italian air; it was hot. The Baroness fumbled at her neck — as incapable, faced with a bow, of untying as of tying; Alan, helpfully pulling at a ribbon's-end, felt his fingers brush past swansdown to throat-flesh even softer. Helpfully the Baroness leaned back; naturally her lips parted; and so Alan, (on his honour or not), kissed her.

What surprised him was the businesslike way in which the Baroness kissed him back. She kissed him thoroughly, expertly; then giggled.

"Is Corky still watching you?" giggled the Baroness. "Or Teresa?"

Alan reared up in momentary anger.

"If you must know —" he began; and paused. He had so nearly forgotten his manners as to be about to refer to her husband. But the goddess Aphrodite once embodied in a Midland landlady kindly came to his aid, and the leaf-mould yielded like a spring-mattress as Alan plunged again and again into sun-warmed waters.

41

THE NEXT EVENING he died. No one expected him to die, least of all Alan himself. The letter he wrote in the morning began as a joke, a game to amuse the Baroness because rain was falling.

"You must have a chit," said Alan solemnly.

"A chit? What is that?" asked the Baroness.

"A note," explained Alan, "to give to our advancing victorious armies to show you deserve special consideration for having befriended one of their heroic lads."

He tore a leaf out of his pocket-book and in indelible pencil, while the Baroness looked over his shoulder, began to write.

"*This is to certify that the Baroness San Felipe, at great personal risk —*"

"I think you might put in Enrico too!" said the Baroness.

"Wait," said Alan.

"*— took in and succoured me, Captain Alan Pennon, K.O.Y.L.I., when an injured and escaping P.O.W. To describe this lady's beauty and kindness is beyond my power; let me say only that her hair is like spun sunshine, and her eyes blue as the sea —*"

"Oh, my darling!" cried the Baroness. "But I am old, old!"

"— *and the sweet freshness of her bosom paradise. Let me record,*" wrote Alan steadily, "*what I have been too tongue-tied to tell her, that without knowing it I have loved her all my life; and that to find her again has made that life worth living . . .*"

The Baroness was by this time dissolved in happy tears; she wept again, more bitterly, that same night. — The long downhill run had exhausted Alan more than he knew; his wrenched knee further drained his strength, also he'd made love when he should have been on a stretcher and he had an inherited weak chest. His body had indeed performed for three years far better than could have been expected of it; now, suddenly, it packed up. The maid Carlotta, summoning the Villa's guest to dine, knocked once, twice, then charged into the guest-room, and screeched . . .

There was nothing heroic about Alan in death. He lay curled quite comfortably on the bed — knees to chin, hands crossed shoulder to shoulder, his mouth slightly open. "Oh, see, Enrico, he smiles at us!" sobbed the Baroness. "Look now, and go," instructed her husband. "Carlotta, take your mistress to bed, and fetch me a napkin."

With great gentleness, alone with his guest, the Marchese bound up Alan's jaw. He was so old a man, he had performed the office many times already; for his uncle the Duke, who had so surprisingly come out with Garibaldi, for a cousin a cardinal, and another a Milanese tycoon; for his own first wife the Principessa Anna-Beatrice. So old was the Marchese, in his lifetime he'd bound up the jaws of a good part of Italian history . . .

No less sympathetic were his attentions to Captain Alan Pennon, K.O.Y.L.I. Carlotta, meeting her master's mind, had produced a last crested linen napkin; not even the Cardinal's jaws were more honourably bound.

The interment, on the other hand, was extremely simple. In circumstances which included a swaying battle-front and the state of the weather, the Marchese thought it best to dispense with ceremony; the two ancient retainers, if they hadn't shot Alan, buried him, actually not far from the ruined summer-house, while the Baroness still wept in her room. But the Marchese made up all Alan's papers into a packet, and sealed it with his own signet-ring, to be turned over in due course to the proper victorious authorities.

The old Marchese overlooked nothing. — He always woke early; he had ample time, next morning, before even Carlotta stirred, to pay a visit to his wife's bedside. As he had expected, the latter, after crying herself to sleep, still slept. She slept in fact soundly; a cheek still tear-stained, even as the Marchese watched, burrowed further into the pillow; did she sob, or snore? "Like a child!" thought the Marchese. "Like a child . . ."

He sat beside her, watching and musing, until he heard Carlotta's step; then girt his dressing-gown about him afresh and emerged, as Carlotta could not fail to observe and report, from his wife's room. The heirless Marchese was a very gallant, also practical, old man.

42

"IF IT HAD been an artery," said Cook solemnly, "we'd have lost you, Mr. Weaver."

"That's right, be cheerful," said Weaver. "Where's the perishing Tray?"

It wasn't an artery he'd cut, out in the woods, but the gash across his left thumb was beyond treatment by Elastoplast: it needed Dr. James and five stitches. Mr. Weaver sat to be sewn up on a kitchen-chair, putting on a remarkable display of unflinchingness, and capped it by immediately afterwards serving refreshments to Cathy and Dr. James by the hall fire. It was one of the best entries he'd ever made; he somehow managed to combine the aspects of perfect butler and Waterloo veteran. His exit was practically the retreat from Corunna.

"Wonderful old chap," said Dr. James, looking after him. "But then the country's chock-a-block with wonderful old chaps. At that guest-house in Chard, for instance, I've a patient getting on for eighty who turns out ditch-digging. — I dare say Lady Jean knows him?" added Dr. James. "Sir Rowland March; he once governed Malta."

A little sherry spilled from Cathy's glass.

"Not Malta; the Next-door Island."

"Well, somewhere in those parts," said Dr. James — who wouldn't have objected to a reminder that he was a pretty wonderful old chap himself, as indeed he was, doggedly coping with his own and a junior partner's practice at an age little short of the Governor's. The omission on Cathy's part didn't however affect his medical conscientiousness towards her. "Now let's take a look at *you*, young woman," said Dr. James. "Circulation still poor?"

"I expect so," said Cathy. "How is he? You said he was your patient."

"Sir Rowland? Digitalis in small doses, but essentially propped up on his last legs by ditch-digging," said Dr. James. "Why don't we ever see you in the village, knitting socks in the Church hall?"

"I can't knit," said Cathy.

"Miss Palmer would be only too glad to teach you. Aggie Palmer," recalled Dr. James appreciatively, "has to date knitted four hundred and three pairs — a message of encouragement, also some slight propaganda for the Labour Party, I understand stiffening each toe."

"I haven't time," said Cathy. "It's a big house."

Dr. James looked down at the small fire flickering between them; across at the Bible-box, dustless, even polished. He had practised in Wellscombe all his life, like his father before him.

"One way or another," agreed Dr. James. "I'll send you a tonic."

Chard was little over twenty miles away. But there was no direct bus-service, and no Henry to drive a car, and, in any case, no petrol. Cathy could still have tramped the distance in two days, if necessary sleeping rough, like a tramp, overnight. Only she was too tired.

Mr. Weaver however took on a new lease of life. His narrow escape — for the myth soon arose that it had

226

been an artery indeed he'd cut — and the consequent opportunity for a display of unflinchingness, pepped him up. He stayed awake over the chess-board and beat Cathy three times running, bullied Cook into serving fish-curries instead of fish-pies, and answered the telephone with almost all his old brio.

"Blow me if here isn't another," reported Weaver cheerily, his left, still-bandaged hand cupped over the mouthpiece. "Lump in the throat and asking for her ladyship . . ."

"This time you can handle it yourself," said Cathy. "Unflinchingly. Anyway, there can't be another. There was only one."

"So far as we know," suggested Weaver.

"I know," said Cathy. "A widow bird sat mourning for her mate."

"Drove an ambulance."

"Don't argue, see who it is."

"No need to be curt, dear," rebuked Mr. Weaver, and switched back to his official voice. "May I have your name, madam?"

"But I've told you!" cried Muriel. "This is Mrs. Maclaren — "

"One of the Scotch lot," reported Weaver. "Wha' d'ye ken's wi' Wallace bled the noo?"

"Just to stop you clowning," said Cathy wearily, "all right, I'll take it."

2

It was some dozen years since she had heard her sister's voice, but she recognized it immediately. So did Muriel recognize Cathy's, and even at such a moment of distress summoned all her old conscientious kindness.

227

"Cathy! How nice to be talking to you again! How are you?" exclaimed Muriel gallantly. "Can I have a word with Lady Jean?"

"She isn't here," said Cathy. "How are Archy and Anna?"

"Splendid," said Muriel. "Anna's a sergeant."

"I know," said Cathy. "She came to see me."

"Really? She never said so," said Muriel. "When will Lady Jean be back?"

"I've no idea," said Cathy.

At the other end of the line Muriel thrust a hand desperately into her husband's. She had waited to telephone until after seven not only to take advantage of cheaper rates but also to have his support. Archy himself was much moved, as he contemplated a promising career in Barclays Bank so abruptly terminated; but he felt far more for his wife than for his sister-in-law.

"Leave it to me, darling," he said firmly, and taking over the receiver. "Listen, Cathy: I'm afraid there's bad news. Your sister wanted to get Lady Jean to break it to you, but as she can't I know you'll be brave . . ."

"Is it Tommy Bamber?" asked Cathy.

"*Who?*"

"Then it must be Alan," said Cathy. "Is it Alan?"

"In Italy," said Archy. ("I'm afraid she's knocked out," he added, to Muriel. "Why on earth think of Tommy Bamber?" "Because she didn't want to think of Alan," sobbed Muriel. "*I* can understand!") — "Is there anyone with you?" asked Archy anxiously.

"Certainly, sir," said Weaver, taking over in turn. "Do I gather Miss Pennon has suffered a loss?"

"Her brother," said Archy — relieved to hear a masculine voice. "My wife and I have just had the sore news her young brother's been killed in Italy. Is there anyone there who can look to her?"

"Or tell her to come home!" cried kind Muriel.

The words were so distinctly audible, even before Archy transmitted them Weaver had turned to watch Cathy's face. He held the receiver balanced on his palm midway between them, not actually proffering it, rather holding it ready for acceptance if she wished. But Cathy violently shook her head.

"Miss Pennon thanks you and sends love," said Weaver formally. "But the Family too has recently suffered a similar bereavement, and she feels her place is here."

3

"Bite on it, dear," said Mr. Weaver. "Chew on the bullet. It's the only way — apart from clowning."

Cathy, crouched on the lowest step of the great stair, let him press her head between her knees. As Mr. Weaver sensibly remarked, we didn't want to faint.

"And in sunny Italy," encouraged Mr. Weaver — his old joints creaking as he stooped beside her — "by all accounts nice and dry. I was at Passchendaele. Lutterel, you mayn't know it, was at Passchendaele too."

"I often wondered," gasped Cathy, "why he let you get away with all that port."

"What a cruel mind you have," rebuked Mr. Weaver, "for such a nice poker-player! — There wouldn't be mud, now, in Italy."

"No; sun," said Cathy.

"Which was a thing always got under my skin," recalled Mr. Weaver thoughtfully, "at gay cocktail-parties. *Here's mud in your eye!* they'd squeal, the silly bas-

tards. '*In your eye-sockets*,' I wanted to say. Even
stretcher-bearers couldn't pick where they trod. Now
your brother, dear, may've died clean as a whistle in the
arms of some lovely signorina . . ."

Cathy was more fortunate than the Maclarens
guessed, in having as consoler a butler who'd been at
Passchendaele, and who could when necessary clown.

4

"Try not to cry so, darling," said Archy. "Think how
proud of him your father would have been . . ."

"Yes, he would, wouldn't he?" sobbed Muriel, but a
little consoled. "He tried so hard, I can remember, to
join up! Alan tied a Union Jack to the laburnum . . .
Darling, how can Cathy *bear* not to be with us now?"

"You must be proud of her too," said Cathy's brother-
in-law firmly, "standing by at the Manor."

Muriel wiped her eyes.

"Good Cathy!" she murmured, almost in the accents
of Lady Jean. "Even after Miss Allen's, I'd never have
believed she could turn out so conscientious!"

43

AS THE WAR ended what Cathy was chiefly was tired. Her lot, by the national standard, hadn't been a particularly arduous one, while so far as material comfort went she had endured considerably less hardship than, for example, the Baroness. She had always worn leather shoes. The deprivation of a *mondaine* society, to the Baroness just as horrid as the deprivation of olive-oil, to Cathy meant nothing. Nor had she seen a lover lying dead in a guest-room immediately before dinner. But what she lacked was the Italian's bounce. The Baroness, or Marchesa, had in fact never looked better or fresher than at the Roman holiday made of her first-born's christening . . .

2

Returned to the arms of a smiling mama, the infant Enrico-Umberto-Jesu-Maria stared up gravely at the surrounding circle of his new relations: a whole aristocratic clan had turned out to enjoy a first post-war fiesta, also to congratulate the San Felipes on their unexpected happiness. The blue-eyed babe was indeed scrutinized with more than usual interest, particularly by the women. "Heavens, how *fair* he is!" cried Cousin Pauline. "He takes after his mother," said the Marchese blandly. "He has even his mother's eyes . . ." "*We* are Venetians," reminded one of the Marchesa's aunts. ("Here comes the Doge!" murmured Pauline aside to her husband. "Who was simply the *gros industriel* of the age," murmured her husband back — sniping at once at Tia Margarita and a second-cousin Milanese tycoon.) "My poor Pauline!" cried the sharp-eared old aunt. "What is this I hear of your taking in dressmaking?" "My little boutique on the Via Veneto?" smiled Pauline. "One must find oneself some sort of occupation, in these wretched times!" "Which die like flies, those little boutiques!" observed the equally sharp-eared tycoon. "There are always good works, charities," pointed out Tia Margarita severely, "with which to occupy oneself!" "No doubt you, dear aunt, have let your villa to the American Red Cross for nothing?" suggested Pauline's husband . . .

It was a splendid party, full of such interesting cross-currents, as around an embroidered pillow the Marchesa's relations on the one hand (delighted at her producing an heir) and the Marchese's on the other (chagrined at losing the pickings of an heirless estate) reciprocally smiled and sniped. The whiff of internecine warfare — so much more stimulating to an Italian than any common front against a foreign foe — animated one and all. All enjoyed themselves extremely. As for Enrico-Umberto-Jesu-Maria, long before the party broke up he was sound asleep upon the bosom of a wet-nurse, innocently and happily unaware of his complicated heritage.

44

IF CATHY WAS tired, so were Mr. Weaver, after his brief renaissance, and Cook tired. All England was tired; almost too tired to celebrate victory. (Rather, survival.) Even Lady Jean, returning at last from London, looked haggard. But the beautiful bone-structure of her skull was still lovelier than any plump cheek of marble cherub, as Cathy against her will was forced to recognize — Lady Jean leaning against the mantel, looking about her, gently sighing . . .

"Alas!" sighed Lady Jean (probably the only woman of her generation who could sigh alas and get away with it.) "Alas, good Cathy! Falling leaf and fading tree!"

"That's 'Tosti's Good-bye,' " said Cathy.

"You always know everything!" said Lady Jean. "It's run in my head all day. How does the next bit go?"

"Lines of white on a sullen sea," supplied Cathy, "shadows falling on you and me."

"Then I've been too dismal," decided Lady Jean, "because I'm actually going to stay with Elspet in Miami. Of course there'll still be the flat in Westminster, and Mr. Lutterel can fight his next election from the dower-house — where how glad I am now we *didn't* find another tenant!"

Cathy couldn't believe it. Familiar as she was with her employer's roundabout approach to anything disagreeable, she still couldn't believe that the Manor was going to be shut. — Or not permanently; perhaps only until after the excursion to Miami. But her employer's next sigh was more explicit.

"The National Trust!" sighed Lady Jean. "The National Trust simply *adores* wattle-and-daub! Or perhaps a very chi-chi finishing school; wouldn't it be nice, good Cathy, to think of the dear old place ringing with fresh young voices?"

They stood one on either side of the hearth. Cathy, looking down into it, could almost identify the big central log as one of the last brought in by Mr. Weaver before his accident. Even half-charred it was still, as Cook had observed, quite a monster . . .

"So the fire's been kept in for nothing?"

"It really has?" exclaimed Lady Jean. "You didn't light it just for me? You really kept it *in?*"

"I and Mr. Weaver," said Cathy. "He cut the wood."

"Who I suppose will have to be pensioned off," meditated Lady Jean, "along with Cook. Good Cathy, what a comfort to know that all *you* need is a reference!"

"I can see why Mr. Lutterel didn't come," said Cathy.

"He's on an extremely urgent Committee," explained Lady Jean. "Something to do with post-war rationing. — Of course you must have saved a small fortune here, but if you *do* want a reference —"

"I want nothing from you at all," said Cathy.

"— how glowing it will be!" congratulated Lady Jean. "What did you say?"

"That I want nothing from you at all," repeated Cathy. "I've made mistake after mistake all my life,

but never a worse one than when I thought you were
the Madonna —"

"Really? How sweet!" murmured Lady Jean.

"— when you're simply a bitch. As Elspet by all accounts is too," added Cathy, "a lass o' her ain pedigree . . ."

For a moment Lady Jean couldn't believe it either.
Then she recalled a whole series of oddities in Cathy's
behaviour, and regretfully concluded that her attendant
sprite had been drinking again. But at least she was
saved a certain amount of bother.

"I must ask you to leave at once," said Lady Jean,
"and *without* a reference. Where you'll go I'm afraid I
can't be concerned —"

"To Chard," said Cathy.

2

With the complicity of Mr. Weaver she left her box to be
sent after her. She couldn't write any labels because she
didn't know where she was bound, beyond Chard; wasn't
certain even of her first stage, since according to Mr.
Weaver, Chard abounded in guest-houses. "The Moorings for one," meditated Mr. Weaver, "which out of
sight and smell of the sea I must say sounds a bit
ersatz. What's that bigger one, Cook, where they've
Poles in the kitchen?"

"The Warren," supplied Cook, "and you mean where
they *had* Poles, Mr. Weaver. Then there's Greensleeves
and The Magnolias —"

"None what you might call five-star," checked Mr.
Weaver. " 'May as well take pot-luck, dear . . .'"

Cathy could of course have telephoned all round;
what prevented her was the irrational fear that the Gov-

ernor might answer in person. She didn't wish to speak to him first over the telephone, but face to face: literally confronting him. — The thought occurred to ring up Dr. James, but the bell echoed in an empty surgery. (Dr. James was in fact the breadth of the parish away delivering a little half-Devonian Mickhailovski; as after the Armada, as after the incursion of the Huguenots, England's sluggish, doggedly heroic blood-stream was being injected with a new strain.) Cathy held on until Mr. Weaver, keeping watch, signalled Lady Jean emergent upstairs; but she would have had to hold on till midnight . . .

"Give us a kiss, dear, ere you depart," said Mr. Weaver.

Cathy gave him not one kiss but four, two on each cheek, and kissed Cook as well, before with but an overnight-bag setting out across country.

3

"I sometimes ask myself," said Cook.

"Don't over-tax your mind," said Mr. Weaver, grimly checking the silver in the green baize bags.

"I sometimes ask myself," repeated Cook stubbornly, "who we've had here."

"A damn good poker-player," said Mr. Weaver.

45

CATHY AS IT happened had neither to tramp two days nor to sleep rough overnight; she hitched a lift on an A.T.S. lorry only half-a-mile outside Wellscombe —

("We're definitely not supposed to," protested its driver, "unless in uniform."

"Darling Peggy, don't be so *regimental!*" fluted a finishing-school accent from the rear. "Isn't the war *over?*")

— and was at Chard by no more than late afternoon on that same day.

Everything shone. All greenery of tree and hedgerow was fully out, but still fresh: under the sweet June sun at once vivid and translucent. A flat elder-flower was a paten of polished ivory, an arching spray of wild rose bore discs of mother-of-pearl; in the grass by the road short-stemmed lesser lovely weeds scattered particles of bright gold. — Cathy still couldn't identify half of them, all she was certain of were dandelions — each a formal miniature sun in itself; but of these she picked first one or two, then more and more, until as she entered the drive to The Moorings she was carrying almost a small bouquet. It indeed smelled no more agreeably than had a wreath of heather from a fishmonger's, but as all brides are beautiful so are all bouquets, and only when the proprietress of The Moorings answered so disagreeably did Cathy let her dandelions drop.

"Sir Rowland March? Not staying *here*," snapped the proprietress. "And I'm afraid we're quite full . . ."

Cathy sensed her rain-coat, bare head and overnight-bag (even without a handful of dandelions) making a poor impression; realized that without meaning to she probably looked like a tramp indeed. Before attempting The Warren she made some slight effort to tidy herself — so successfully, she was taken for an applicant to the post of waitress. "Never mind about experience!" cried the proprietress of The Warren, almost before Cathy opened her mouth. "Just come and muck in! Have you a dog?"

"No," said Cathy. "Is Sir Rowland March — ?"

"Because you could *bring* a dog," persuaded the proprietress. "We'd *welcome* a dog — if you'd be on duty from four till nine?"

"I haven't got a dog," said Cathy patiently. "Is Sir Rowland — ?"

"Even a pony?" suggested the proprietress desperately. "If you've a pony, it could run in the paddock . . ."

"Sir Rowland March," repeated Cathy. "Is he staying here?"

"No, he isn't," said the disappointed proprietress. "Sir Rowland March? I've never heard of him."

Cathy strongly suspected this to be untrue. She had Dr. James's word that the Governor lodged somewhere in Chard, and he could hardly fail to be a conspicuous figure there. (She was in fact more than right. The Governor had actually stayed at The Warrens for some months, before being driven away by an inadequate supply of bath-water.) Cathy had no intention of abandoning the search, but it was fortunate for her spirits, after being taken first for a tramp, then for an unemployed waitress, that at The Warren's gate she encountered Captain Powell.

2

What Cathy immediately perceived of him was that he looked like the sort of man the Governor would know; reciprocally, the sort of man who'd know the Governor. Captain Powell in shabby slacks and out-at-elbows poacher's jacket was indeed about as trampishly got up as Cathy; but she hadn't spent her early youth on the Next-door Island for nothing, and her second perception, strengthening the first, was that he was Service. Point-blank —

"I'm looking for the Governor," said Cathy.

Captain Powell for his part accepted her rather wild accost with true naval coolness. — At heart he was a gun-boat man, ever ready aye ready to ship any pro-British sheikh out of trouble and if possible to Sandhurst; but always very, very coolly. Such happy days being long past, he found a slight pleasure, a welcome exercise of a disused special talent, even in keeping cool in the face of a dishevelled young woman in a country lane.

"What do you want him for?" he asked cautiously.

For Cathy by this time was looking not only wild, but desperate; and though Captain Powell felt no particular liking for Sir Rowland — hadn't he had two Fuzzy-Wuzzies flogged to death? — a certain masculine solidarity operated. It in fact crossed his mind, though he wasn't normally imaginative, that this fierce young woman might be the Governor's natural daughter, come to demand provision, or an inheritance. There was no likeness; his only ground for the fantasy was a common air of having somehow gone off the rails. The impression was still so strong, when Captain Powell remembered the Governor's age, and how modestly he quartered at The Magnolias, his impulse was to save the old chap from any possible consequences.

"I want to talk to him," said Cathy. "That's all: to talk to him."

"He's doddery," said Captain Powell. (Himself a full two years the Governor's junior.) "He doesn't remember a name or place."

"I think he might remember me," said Cathy. "I was a Bear. At his children's Fancy Dress ball at Government House."

Unexpectedly, it worked. Captain Powell reflected that even the Governor, odd fish as he was, would hardly have introduced his natural daughter at an official tamasha; also that the old boy might rather enjoy such harmless reminiscences; so he directed Cathy to The Magnolias.

She this time had no need to make preliminary enquiries, also unscrupulously presented herself as a caller from Wellscombe Manor. "Those dear Lutterels!" exclaimed the proprietress, who had once glimpsed Lady Jean in the distance at a Conservative fête. — "I'd take you myself," she apologized (short-staffed as her sister of The Warren, but gallantly concealing floury hands), "if I weren't expecting an important phone call — but just go through the grounds and you'll find Sir Rowland by the lake."

46

IT WAS NO more a lake than the garden and orchard behind the guest-house were grounds. It was a pond. (How diminished all the Governor's appurtenances!) But he himself, even from the back, Cathy recognized at once; his head not much more grizzled, only a little more sunken between shoulders not much more hunched. He occupied a sagging rustic bench rather too low for him; alongside grew an ancient fig-tree, propped on crutches, in the branches of which, looking almost equally out of place, clambered an ancient parrot with an evil eye.

Cathy rounded the seat. Observing the approach of a female, Sir Rowland fumbled with the rug over his knees in a courteous attempt to rise. The effort was so obvious, Cathy quickly sat down herself — possibly giving the impression of a new fellow-guest; for His Excellency's courtesy now extended to include a warning.

"Watch out that bird doesn't bite you," said Sir Rowland.

His voice was still deep, but he took a little time to articulate. — Overhead the parrot cocked a red-rimmed eye and chattered something altogether incomprehensible.

"How old is it?" asked Cathy foolishly.

"Old as the hills," said the Governor. "I dare say as old as I am."

He relapsed into silence, gazing out under hooded lids across the pond — about fifteen feet wide, bounded on the further side by a small shrubbery. After the Mediterranean, the approaches to a railway-station: now over a duck-pond brooded the wise Ulysses . . .

"Remember me," said Cathy abruptly. "I'm Cathy Pennon, but I was a Bear. My sister was a Contadina, and Alan was an Elf, but I was a Bear. On the Island, a long time ago, when you were Governor."

Without shifting his gaze —

"I have been governor of many islands," said His Excellency.

"The Next-door Island," prompted Cathy, "at the children's Fancy-dress Ball. You took me out on the balcony. Don't you remember at all?"

"No," said the Governor. "I'm sorry; but I'm old."

"I remember," said Cathy. "I've always remembered; what you told me, out on the balcony."

"I have the habit," reflected the Governor dispassionately, "of saying too much and too little. What was it I told you?"

Cathy moistened her lips. She hadn't been aware that they were dry, but now she needed to moisten them.

"Always to hold the thread to the sun."

"That was at least reasonable," said the Governor. "Look out for the bird."

The parrot had indeed clambered down onto his shoulder — its beak at the ready, its eye on the new-comer.

"But it's been no use," said Cathy. "And now I think perhaps I never knew what you meant."

"Why, affection," said the Governor. "Love, if you like, but at any rate affection. That's what we Anglo-Saxons need."

"Then I've been wrong all my life," said Cathy.

"If you have never loved," agreed the Governor, for the first time turning to look at her. "All your life, you say? How old are you?"

"Forty," said Cathy. — She couldn't believe it herself, that she was forty. Where had forty years gone?

"A child," said the Governor. "Perhaps I do remember you — or some child, on the Next-door Island. I had a house there," said the Governor suddenly.

"Of course," said Cathy. "Government House."

Under his grizzled moustache Sir Rowland as suddenly smiled.

"Not that great white elephant: a house of my own. A private establishment, in the Strada San Giorgio."

Cathy cast her mind back intently. She recalled such a street by name; and Jacko's reference to it — how long ago? — outside a door in Soho; with some sort of meaning, again, she hadn't grasped . . .

"He wasn't altogether a fool, my aide-de-camp," meditated the Governor. "At least he knew how to cover up."

"I know he covered up the tapestries," said Cathy uncertainly. "Alan told me."

"Alan?"

"My brother who came as an Elf. He's been killed in Italy."

"Italy or the Dardanelles," said the Governor absently. "Extraordinarily enough, I've still the key."

Extraordinarily indeed, from under the rug, from a

pocket that sagged like Mr. Lutterel's, he produced a crook of hand-wrought iron; held it balanced on his palm. Upon the slip of ivory attached Cathy could just discern a number, and his name. — The parrot made to take it in its beak.

"Who lives there now?" asked Cathy.

"I imagine it's empty," said the Governor. "She should have filled it with relations and a smell of garlic, but she died, poor lovely creature; so I suppose it's empty. — As soon as the sun's down we'll be cold," said the Governor, painfully beginning to lever himself up from the bench.

"It won't be down for hours," said Cathy. "It's June."

"There's still a chill in the air," said the Governor.

His old hand, his old foot, fumbled with the rug; but at last his old eyes bent on Cathy their full power of stored experience and wisdom. He also, at last, genuinely recognized her.

"There's never been an Empire yet," said His Excellency, "the sun didn't set on. Perhaps I should have told you that too. It's a time for beginning again."

"Begin again, begin again, begin again!" squalled the parrot.

"But I'm too old!" cried Cathy.

"Nonsense," said the Governor. "You're still a child. It's I who'm too old — even to cherish a memory. *Basta!*" said the Governor.

With which, now on his feet, he made a motion to chuck the key into the pond. That he paused was probably due to the arthritis in his hands making any swift movement difficult; or perhaps the iron had its own mana, like the Bible-box at Wellscombe, like the key Mr. Lutterel carried. — The Governor paused; his eye fell on Cathy again. Though he'd recognized her, it was still but vaguely. He didn't remember he'd ever called her a young Marid. Purely from the indifference of great age, the key balanced on his palm —

"Unless you've a use for it?" said the Governor.

SHARP, MARG

THE SUN IN

LITTLE BROW